Sylvie's Escape

Mary Catelli

Published by Wizard's Wood Press, 2026.

SYLVIE'S ESCAPE

First edition. March 12, 2026.

ISBN: 978-1-942564-81-2

Written by Mary Catelli.

Chapter 1: The Kitten

Sylvie turned from the window. "I'm going down to the garden," she announced.

The maids barely nodded as they put away her clothes and made a great pother of how cold it would be, here at this castle in the mountains, and whether they could get her warmer clothes, and how hard it would be.

"That it would be an honor to serve as the princess's seamstress is no help," said Meg, without a glance at the princess herself, "if there is no seamstress to honor!"

The sound fell behind as Sylvie frolicked along the hallway and down the stairs in a way that would have her governess remind her that she was a princess and almost grown-up—if Lady Richeza had watched instead of worrying about the wardrobe.

Sylvie giggled and slipped out, into chilly air where stands of wild roses abounded in white flowers and sweet scent. Walkways of grass curled between the rose bushes. To her left, a gate to a courtyard showed irises and tulips in a walled garden. She skipped off to her right, where the rose bushes grew.

An old man stood among the bushes, scything the grass, but he shoved the scythe under his arm and pulled off his cap, and said, "So this is our imperiled princess, come for refuge."

Sylvie hesitated.

"There are so many tales, Your Highness. The children even gabble of dragons."

Sylvie laughed. "No, not a dragon. A duke." She scowled. "His coat of arms does have a dragon on it."

He shook his head. "Even a child should be able to tell the difference between a coat of arms and a real dragon."

Sylvie laughed again, and sobered. "Then—he's hiring mercenaries. Captain Redcloak's. Except they aren't enough to face my father's men.

So they were going to capture me." She looked down at her hands. Her mother had hidden her in a room without windows and allowed only the most trusted servants in. "So—my father sent me here, far from them."

"And we will be glad to guard you," said a woman.

Sylvie started. The gardener looked between the rose bushes and nodded to a newcomer. An old woman hobbled up. She wore a red shawl over her white hair and bore a basket. She hailed the gardener as old Hobbe, he greeted her as Jilliane, and she smiled on Sylvie.

"Such lovely blond hair. Like Queen Angelique."

Sylvie's hand went to her hair. At court, when people talked of her hair, they spoke how she took after, not her mother Queen Cecelia, but her grandmother Queen Helena. Not the legendary Queen Angelique. Her tongue touched her lips.

The woman's smile deepened. "I have brought a *gift*."

Sylvie tilted her head to one side.

Jilliane laughed, the wrinkles of her face crinkling. "A kitten of Queen Angelique. They still breed true around here."

"More or less," said Hobbe, shifting his scythe.

"Too true," said the old woman. "But it is in many things that the true kittens show themselves." She put down the basket and started to open its lid.

A loud merow came from within. Sylvie blinked. A bolt of white darted from the basket toward Sylvie, who dropped to her knees to scoop the kitten up. Pure white, with blue eyes, and rubbing against her shoulder. . . .

"Aye, that's the old story," said Hobbe. "The kittens always know who they want."

"It's a proper Queen Angelique's kitten, too," said the old woman. "Will hunt the mice in the larder and not the birds outside your window."

"Queen Angelique's hair and Queen Angelique's kitten," said Hobbe with satisfaction.

"Oh, yes," said Jilliane. "Queen Helena had Queen Angelique's hair, but no Queen Angelique's kitten. Not like this one."

And the kitten was entirely white without a fleck of other color to it, with those ice-blue eyes—"Snowfall," Sylvie said. "She's named Snowfall."

#

The book lay open before her, and Sylvie sighed and contemplated turning the page. Her father had not exaggerated when he apologized for the library. Silly chronicles telling of the days of Queen Friederike and making her out to be either a villain of deepest dye, or an angel of sweetness and purity, and all of it as dry as dust.

She sat back and stretched her arms. If the writer was being shameless, he should at least make the tale adventurous.

Then she lowered her arms. When her mother had made sure she had Lady Richeza to serve as her a new governess, since Lady Dagmar had left before the journey to the castle, Sylvie had said that they sent her for her safety not her studies, and her mother had smiled.

Snowfall meowed. Sylvie blinked. The kitten pushed at the page with a paw.

Sylvie laughed. "I'd rather go scrub dishes, but I must finish reading. Even if she's just assigning books to keep me busy." She sighed. "Even though there aren't so much as better tales about the mountains that the books I read back down at the seashore."

She scratched Snowfall behind the ears. Or go sew, she'd rather do that, though they had found a seamstress. A breeze made the shadows of leaves dance on the floor. She could go into the garden as long as she read the rest of the lesson later.

She couldn't go too far. Not even to the kitchen, though the kitchen maids were ready with scraps for Snowfall. The promised visitors might, after all, arrive. She glanced down. Maids had dressed her in a white undergown with a gold-trimmed overgown of blue, and they had cooed over brushing out her tow hair as if it were spun gold, so they expected important visitors.

Still, they could see her from the window as long as she stayed in the garden.

She scooped up Snowfall, who purred in the crook of her elbow, and slipped out the back door, through the stand of apple trees past blooming but without so much as green apples, into sunlight and flower beds where early irises bloomed among the late tulips.

Snowfall meowed and leapt to the ground. Sylvie laughed. "Are there mice in the tulips? Or rabbits in the irises?"

Snowfall prowled onward.

"Snowfall," she called.

Her tail twitching, the kitten poked her nose into the tulip bed.

"Snowfall. I can't go chasing after you. Not too far."

Snowfall half vanished behind tulips. She had come before when called—generally. Sylvie bit her lip, glanced at her skirt, and gathered it up. Grass stains would be bad, but—how could she let a Queen Angelique's kitten get lost in the woods? "Snowfall," she called again, "Snowfall."

She had a glimpse of white among the purple and green by the wall and ran, her skirts slapping against her knees, but Snowfall was already by the gate and wriggling through the lattice work to reach the roses.

She dropped her skirts to unlatch the gate and follow. In that time, Snowfall vanished into the rose bushes. A petal as white as the cat fell before her. Sylvie fought down shouting, before her servants found her, and called softly, "Snowfall."

Snowfall darted between two bushes. Sylvie started toward her when shouts rose from the castle. She cringed and ducked behind the nearest rose bush.

The leaves hid her from the castle and the castle's servants, but from there, she could see the road. Soldiers rode on it. Not her father's soldiers but men in drab red uniforms. Captain Redcloak's men.

When the branches of a bush struck her back, she realized she had backed away.

In the bright sunlight, her thoughts were frozen. Then, slowly, they moved. She had backed away, but not far enough.

She gathered her skirts again and ran away. A white and blue dress could be seen easily from far off. She had to run very far.

Snowfall bounded out of a white rosebush and ran alongside her down the paths. At the brink of the woods, Snowfall ran ahead, darting under fallen branches and about stands of ferns. Sylvie ran after. Any direction away was good, up hill or down, crossing a muddy stream on stones with great care because a fall might hurt her so she could not run, flitting about trees that were not thick enough to hide her.

She was breathing hard when the shouts came after her—so muffled with distance that she dared look back. She could barely make out the castle through the trees. Then she looked down, at her skirt. They didn't need to make out her, just her gown.

She drew a deep breath. She would be out of breath as soon as she ran again, and she might have to run.

Snowfall meowed.

"I had best go downhill," she said. "Out of sight."

Snowfall meowed with approval and walked off. Downhill. Sylvie followed. The way was steep, and she walked with care. Snowfall darted ahead a bit, and Sylvie blinked. White stood ahead.

Birches, of course. Her breath gusted out. Snowfall already delicately picked her way over the forest floor, and Sylvie inched down the slope. She reached the birches, with their white bark and their pale green leaves. The sunlight that shone through the leaves turned green the way it did under no other trees. The ferns and moss grew uncommonly thickly here, and a stream ran through it, glittering in the sunlight.

On a hunt, if she had gotten lost, she would stay still so that she would not go in circles about rescuers. But—she gulped—no rescuers would come to save her.

Though the mercenaries had come so far for her that they would certainly look as soon as they realized she was missing.

Snowfall ambled about the birch grove, around the thick trucks of the old birches. With a sigh, Sylvie picked her direction. The stream ran downhill. It would not go in circles, and so she had some hope of getting away.

Within a few minutes, she reached the edge of the birch grove. She looked at the dead leaves ahead and walked on. Meowing, Snowfall ran ahead.

Nothing showed any sign of shelter or food, as far as she could see. It was already after noon, but, she told herself stoutly, she had hours before dark.

She walked on, staying far enough from the stream to avoid slipping in mud or having to clamber over rocks. Birds sang in the trees, and the stream babbled, and Sylvie told herself that the mercenaries would be loud enough for her to hear.

She faced no thickets, at least, to whip their branches back at her if she released them before she escaped their reach. She wished she had boots, though. It might be safer to climb on the rocks if her shoes could endure it.

A squirrel ran through the dead leaves, making them rustle.

Down and down and down, through stands of oaks where acorns rolled underfoot, through groves of beech with silvery bark.

The sun inched across the sky.

Down and down and down, through long stretches of maples. She stopped now and again, and Snowfall circled her feet, and a minute later, she walked on.

Dark trees appeared ahead: a stand of fir trees, too thick for her to see the other side of them. The stream flowed through it.

Snowfall stopped and meowed. Sylvie walked on. Snowfall stayed close by her feet, which did not hearten her. The stream flowed steadily, almost flat, no longer gurgling. She thought that nothing grew in the shade of the firs, it was so dark, but she could not see clearly.

She inched in. Snowfall was a brightness in the gloom, padding ahead, but she had to watch her footing. Nothing grew here, not even pale lichens on the trunks, but the forest floor was thick with fallen needles and firs' tiny cones, awkward to step on.

The edge of the firs fell behind her, and a splash of light gleamed ahead. She walked toward it. A vast tree had fallen, and though its trunk was overgrown with moss and mushroom, none of the eager saplings had grown enough to fill the gap it had opened.

A sound in the woods made her start. The shadows looked all the darker for having looked at the sunlight. Sylvie's heart hammered as she peered and could not see.

A deer, she told herself. It might be a deer.

Someone came walking toward her. She shrank back.

"Your Highness? Are you lost?" The man stopped, still in the shadows of the firs. "I can get you back to the castle—"

"No!" Her word tore through his, and her hand went to her face.

The man hesitated. Then he took a stride forward so that the sunlight shone on him: a woodsman, dressed browns and grays and russets, his hair light brown, and not really a man, though older than she was. He went down on one knee.

"Your Highness." His voice was very formal. "How may I aid you?"

Chapter 2: The Forest

The way through the forest was still a long walk. Snowfall frolicked about, now and again chasing squirrels and dead leaves. Hendrick sometimes took Sylvie's hand to help her over the uneven spots, where rocks were outcroppings on the steep slope. After a time, he stopped dropping her hand when they were over the rough spots.

She was glad of that when he led her down a steep slope. It had no rocks. The tree roots spread about the dirt, and she carefully moved her foot from one to the other as if they were steps, however awkwardly placed. Hendrick held her hand and, in a low voice, pointed out new roots. He took care with his own footing. Snowfall pranced ahead, stepping lightly, and Sylvie tried to not envy her.

They passed a stand of ferns that rose nearly to her head, and the forest floor ahead came clearer. A stream ran down ahead of them. She turned her attention back to her steps.

They had climbed three quarters of the slope before she saw that a cliff loomed beside them. She looked away but still felt a spurt of fright.

"We're near the bottom," Hendrick assured her. "It levels out here." He glanced at the stream. "Be careful not to step in the mud and leave footprints."

She blinked and felt silly. "I only thought about slipping."

He grinned. "That's wise to avoid, too." Then he steadied her again.

Finally, they reached the bottom and stood on level ground. Next to them, a jumble of gray rocks bore patches of moss and hollows filled with dead leaves. The stream, smaller than the earlier one, gurgled through it. Sylvie picked her way with care, stepping on stones to avoid the mud.

Hendrick waved at the rocks. "Sit here."

A protest jumped to her mouth, but she choked it down. Lady Dagmar had warned her, often, about there being no point in having servants who knew things if you knew better than them.

Sunlight shone as flecks of brightness over the rocks. It glittered on the stream and danced with the breezes. Snowfall bounded up the rock and looked about inquisitively. Hendrick started to walk toward the cliff. Water spouted from a rock there, and his steps squished through the mud.

The spring that fed the stream, Sylvie realized, even before he took out a water bottle. Snowfall bounded up and lapped at the pool.

"You should drink what you can," said Hendrick. "It's better than carrying it in the bottle." He glanced back. "If this is not enough to support a village, it's more than we can drink dry. If they follow us here, they will find water."

She had to take the bottle in both hands, and when she lifted it to her mouth, the water was icy cold.

After minutes drinking, she said, "You did not fear their following us much. Before. You weren't looking around."

"It would slow us," said Hendrick. "And their red is only a little less conspicuous than that dress you wear, princess. It does not take much looking." He let out his breath. "But the village I lead you to is not much farther by the road."

"Especially since they have horses," said Sylvie, thoughtfully. She drank some more. A bit later, she blinked, and Hendrick took the empty bottle to fill it up again.

"There's a path not far from here," he said. "The way there's not so steep."

Sylvie looked up the slope that they had come down, and giggled. It could not be much steeper. She wondered that they had managed that at all.

#

The way to the path went by stream, and would have been a gentle slope if it weren't for the rocks littering the banks. Snowfall flitted ahead. Now and again, she sat and meowed at Sylvie, then waited until the princess caught up. Hendrick helped her more than once, and once lifted her up to walk past a spread of mud with only his tracks.

She was glad to see the path, beaten earth surrounded by dried leaves. And very few rocks.

Hendrick pointed down the path and soberly said, "That way leads to a village. But do not leave the path."

"If a wolf tells me to leave, I shall run!"

He smiled, briefly, at that. Then he said, "If I tell you to, run. As fast as you can. Without looking back. And without thinking about me."

For a moment she stared at him, and her mouth was dry. He couldn't fight off soldiers for long.

She raised her head. "If we hurry, it will be less likely that I will need to run."

He smiled more heartily at that, and they walked. The path was easier on her feet, and it crossed streams with rocks set as stepping stones, or planks of wood laid across the water.

"Be wary of trees that fall over a waterway," he said. "Still more of fallen trees that cross your way."

"It might be rotten because I do not know how long it has lain there," said Sylvie. "If I step on it, it may fall apart. And then I'd fall over. I could hurt myself."

Hendrick raised an eyebrow. "You seem wise in woodcraft. What else do you know?"

Sylvie hesitated, wondering if he were making fun of her. "Also, I should listen to the woodsmen who know the woods in truth."

Hendrick laughed.

Rocks littered the trail's side. Sometimes cliffs towered above them, on either hand or both, or worse, dropped off below. The worst was when the trail itself passed on the only level part of the slope. Trees growing on the rock were twisted with the effort of growing there, and ferns grew in gaps with stone stark about their green. Sylvie stared ahead.

In due course, the path leveled out, but only when it was already evening, with the sunlight turning orange. Vast trees stood to either side, but sunlight fell on the path itself, here. Snowfall prowled along the edge, sometimes poking her nose into thickets of wildflowers.

Hendrick pointed ahead. "There's the village. We have reached safety."

She had to stand on her tiptoes to see roofs over the brush, but soon she heard voices and, after that, saw cottages with their gardens about them. The clamor in the village grew louder with every step, making Hendrick frown. Then one voice came clear.

"—I thought it was the wisest, with no way to get back in."

Hobbe sounded distraught, she realized. And he was here.

"Soldiers were everywhere, and they were searching everywhere. If Lisette escaped it was a marvel—but for the princess—" His voice broke.

"Perhaps she was helped," said—Jilliane? wondered Sylvie.

"And she was!" called Hendrick grandly.

It drew a few puzzled glances. Then Snowfall darted forward toward the crowd and rubbed against Jilliane's ankles. Jilliane blinked, looked about, and started the exclamations of wonder.

Within a minute, Sylvie found herself in the middle of the villagers, better hidden from the eye than when in the midst of the trees, while they praised Heaven for her safety.

"I'm not safe yet," she said. "Not until the mercenaries leave."

"Not while you're wearing that," said one woman. "Marlene, come here and stand beside her."

A girl with vivid reddish-gold hair stared but scrambled up. About the village, heads nodded sagely. She stood only a little taller than Sylvie. Sylvie gave her a sideways glance, and realized that Marlene glanced at her.

A little child piped up, "That's a *stupid* thing to wear to hide in the woods."

Silence fell.

Sylvie said, "It's the very wisest thing in the world to wear to hide in the woods, because it was what I had on when I learned the mercenaries were already at the castle."

She turned to face the child. He looked at her with enormous eyes. "You fight wars with the army you have, not the army you want. You run away with the clothes you have on, not with the clothes you want to have on."

Murmurs of approval spread, some nodding their heads and saying a right regal answer, and the child's hand went to his mouth.

"But then you change as soon as you can," said the woman. "Marlene, come with me to help."

The two of them bustled her through a cottage garden, indistinct with the light, but sweet smelling. Snowfall darted ahead, toward the dark gap of the doorway. The shadows within held a dull red glow; the fire was all but banked.

A kitten trotted out: a red tabby with only patches of white. Marlene squeaked something about Dawn, but the two kittens sniffed at each other and, after a moment, slipped into the cottage before them.

Even their whiteness was hard to see in the cottage. The woman ordered Marlene to put another log on the fire.

"At least we don't have to worry about whether the clothes are becoming," she muttered, going over to a chest. "And that old Will paid us off in cloth may turn out well after all."

She hefted up the lid. Then she paused, turned to Sylvie and said, "My name is Adelaide, Your—" She scowled.

"Sylvie," said Sylvie firmly.

The woman swallowed and said, "Sylvie, my name is Adelaide."

"And I'm Marlene!" said the girl.

The kitten Dawn blinked at her and stalked off to sit by the fire.

Then Adelaide took out gowns and dressed Sylvie in green and brown. And white for her shift—orange by firelight, and Sylvie suspected it would be off-white by sunlight. Snowfall pounced now and again on the trailing cloth, but she still managed to try the cloth against herself, to see if the clothes would fit. At least closely enough for a growing girl.

The linen was coarser than her own shift. Which, she told herself, would help hide that she was the princess. She pulled a shift and gown on, and watched in silence while Adelaide folded up her own gown and shift and hid them both deep in the chest.

"You'll have to pull back your hair, too," said Adelaide. "No peasant girl will let her hair get in her way all the time."

"They'll know she's not a peasant girl," said a man, filling in the doorway and looking darkly on the room. Adelaide raised an eyebrow, and he came in. "They'll figure out she's new."

"Tell them I'm a cousin who had to come here from having lived with my parents at court," said Sylvie. "Tell them I'm named Sylvie after the princess and I'll tell them how the court's lands are littered with Sylvies and Sylvias and Sylvianas and Sylvios and even Sylvesters!"

"Best if they do not see you at all," said Adelaide.

The man looked grave. "But she had best stay here. If she's wearing Marlene's cast-offs—" He shook his head.

"I'm a cousin," said Sylvie.

Marlene frowned.

"I'm a distant cousin, because—" Sylvie threw her arms out. "—everyone is a distant cousin from far enough back. So you won't be lying."

All three of them looked at her. The man's mouth quirked a little, as if beginning a smile. And then Sylvie yawned.

"You walked all the way from the castle, didn't you?" said Marlene.

"Some of it I ran," said Sylvie.

Marlene giggled. Adelaide smiled a little.

"Food," said the man. "With something to drink. After, bed. The morning is wiser than the evening."

Chapter 3: The Village

Over stew, she learned that the man's name was Otto. They ate by firelight, which left the cottage mostly in shadow.

A knock sounded on the door as she ate another spoonful.

The other three looked up in surprise. Sylvie's spoon froze in midair as she looked from one to the next. Otto called for the visitor to come in.

The door opened for a man, his hair pale but looking reddish by firelight, with a boy nearly grown after him. Not the mercenaries' uniforms. About her, all three eased.

"Be welcome to this house, Master Gregor," said Otto. "And your son."

Sylvie bit her lip, wondering if she knew how to be courteous here. Lady Dagmar had done her best to teach her odd titles and ranks, but she did not remember this man from her lessons. She lowered the spoon. She did not even know whether he was noble. Lady Richeza had not given her lessons about the mountains when they traveled, as Lady Dagmar always had.

Then she blinked, and realized that the boy was Hendrick. She felt her face heating. Ingratitude was worse than ill-manners.

"So you heard our news!" caroled Adelaide. "Of our cousin."

Hendrick started and looked at her, his face blank.

The man blinked. His eyes narrowed, and he slowly looked over all of them. Time enough for Marlene to whisper that he was the Master of the Mountains.

Sylvie winced. So he was noble. Only—not easily placed. Lady Dagmar had hated such titles but taught her as many as she could, and warned her to watch with care, to reckon their place. She was glad of his silence. It gave her a moment to think—and to realize, with relief, that acting like they were in court would betray her if anyone watched.

She shifted a bit. And she needed to act if someone might watch, at any time, to keep the habit.

Then Gregor completed his survey and said, "It occurred to me that the news might have grown garbled. Rumor often does that."

"That can cause ill will," said Otto. "A distant cousin to be sure. Named Sylvie, like the princess. Doing that is common about court, so she says."

"It might be wise to not chatter about the princess," said Sylvie, brightly. "You may think that they never listen to the common folk, but I can tell you, there's many a courtier who can hear whatever is of advantage to him in their talk. Still more the soldiers."

She looked at them both. "I am going to stay here with my cousins. And hold my tongue."

"That will help," said Gregor, his tone measured. "But not suffice."

"Well, then, Gregor," said Adelaide, sounding patient, "I've never known you to say such a thing without having a plan up your sleeve to deal with matter. Spit it out."

"We need to watch the soldiers," said Gregor. "See what they do."

The fire crackled.

"They're watching you," said Sylvie. "They always do. It's more important that they not see anything out of common."

Hendrick said, "They don't know much of what is common about here."

"She's right, though," said Gregor. "There is only so much we can do, but to keep to the common customs will help some. And they have the castle's servants to tell them."

"Or lie to them," said Otto.

In the silence, a log settled deeper into the coals with a sigh.

"Though," said Otto heavily, "the lies might be more dangerous than if they tell the truth."

"But—" It drew every gaze, and Sylvie had to plow on. "They might not know what is common or uncommon, and they might take ordinary things as suspicious. They—I don't know what they would take as ordinary."

"We still have to keep to our work," said Hendrick. Adelaide raised an eyebrow. "And see to it that the mercenaries do harm to no man or woman, child or beast, in the mountains—if we can." He stared straight ahead. "Least of all to the princess, wherever she is."

Sylvie yawned and felt ashamed.

"Let us talk under the stars, then," said Otto, standing up. "Sylvie should rest. She had a long journey."

"But," said Sylvie, "someone should send word to the king."

Gregor looked at her with narrowed eyes, and she blushed.

"If—if there is a way to do it."

Gregor nodded, gravely. Moments later, the door closed behind the men. Sylvie scraped the bowl of the last of her stew. As soon as it was done, Adelaide took the bowl and showed her the bed. She said her prayers and laid down. Snowfall curled up by the fireplace, purring. Adelaide sat at her spinning wheel, and Marlene carding wool, both golden by firelight.

Sylvie yawned. "I can't spin," she said, drowsily. "Lady Dagmar was teaching me, but she didn't get far. I can sew very well."

"Good," said Adelaide. "No one would believe you a cousin if we did not put you to work."

#

There was movement about the room, and Sylvie opened her eyes into her pillow. The light was too dim, it had to be before dawn. The servants should know how to move more quietly.

Then she recognized the pillow. She swallowed. Of course they would be about their work. She should join them, to pass better as their cousin.

At that, she told herself stoutly, as she pushed herself up, word might have come from the castle. Perhaps the mercenaries had left when she wasn't there. She yawned and sat up. The voices outside the cottage sounded excited.

"Lisette is back," said Marlene, happily, from across the room. She closed a jug and came out into the morning light.

"Is she?" said Sylvie. Then she remembered. The seamstress. "That's glorious! Does she have word of the castle? Or did she just escape?"

Marlene grabbed her hand and pulled. Sylvie scampered after to the doorway and out, where the crowd was as large as it had been for Hobbe. Lisette, wrapped in dew-wet shawl, talked of how she hid in back rooms and slipped out.

Marlene stopped. Sylvie stopped with her and did not free her hand. No one noticed them.

"It took long enough to reach the woods," she said. "You didn't want to catch their eye. Especially after Lady Richeza."

"Lady Richeza?"

Sylvie could not pick out the questioner, but Lisette only shook her head sadly. Sylvie scowled.

"Who's she?" whispered Marlene. "This—Richeza?"

"My governess," whispered Sylvie back.

"The soldiers were full of complaints," said Lisette. "She was supposed to lead them to the princess, and they could not find her. The princess, not Lady Richeza. She should have tried hiding herself. She just told them that she knew the princess had been in the library. They hauled her to the ramparts and hung her from them for lying to them."

Sylvie, for a moment, could not breathe. Startled exclamations about the crowd, and they started looking at her.

"She—she was appointed by—" Sylvie swallowed and told herself not say her mother. "—by the queen, because of her relatives." For power, thought Sylvie. An honor for a noble family that was angry with the king. She gulped. Lady Dagmar had begged Queen Cecelia to name Lady Annika to replace her, but her mother had gently said that such favoritism toward their family would be unreasonable.

"Honor truly is dead among them," said one old man. "Betraying the princess by taking a post in her household, to hand her over to her enemies?"

Grim nods, and murmured agreement, seeped through the crowd. Sylvie swallowed. That was just what must have happened.

Snowfall meowed at her feet. Sylvie picked her up, and the kitten rubbed against her face.

"But for our good news," caroled Adelaide. "My distant cousin named her child Sylvie. Like the princess. She can not stay at court any longer, but now that she has to come here, she can sew."

Lisette raised an eyebrow. "Like they do at court? The lady was not pleased with my stitches."

"Oh, yes," said Sylvie. "It was for court. I can sew for it."

"No one'll believe that," said an old woman. "A cousin named Sylvie?"

"Then you need to talk about dragons," said Sylvie. "Or ogres."

Hobbe started to laugh, setting them all off. Sylvie bit her lip. The mercenaries might be willing to take a girl named Sylvie because she *might* be the princess.

"And the king needs to get word." She sighed. "If that can be done. You would know more than I do."

"He's off in the lowlands," grumbled a drab man of grayish brown, from his hair to his shoes.

"He'll come after this," said a fair-haired woman.

"He has to be careful," said Sylvie, with care. "I—the princess would be far worse off as a prisoner if they killed the king. As long as he's king, she's needed to ward him off." She felt very flat. If they killed her father—she did not want to think about that.

"Enough of this," said Adelaide. "There's sewing to be done, and wood to be chopped." She looked about. "And other work, I dare say."

"She can show me how to sew well enough for court!" said Marlene.

Sylvie blinked. She could do it herself—but could she teach it?

"Can she?" said Lisette, looking at Sylvie with new interest.

#

They bustled about with fabric and thread, ignoring her. Marlene seemed as much at loose ends as she was.

Sylvie tried to look about. There was indeed forest on the other side of the valley. Though the valley itself had few trees, the forest wrapped around it. The cottages were high enough on the slope that she could not see down.

"Oh, yes, you have to see what the valley is like!" Marlene grabbed her hand. "Since you haven't been here before."

Marlene hurried down a path to the last cottages. The valley spread before them. It held stands of trees, all orchards, past flowering—and pastures with grazing sheep and fields set with crops. A stream ran down it, with a pool where someone was fishing.

Of course. No matter how much they sold the herbs for, they could not have all their food brought up river to buy.

"We'd better get back," said Marlene. "They'll have the stuff ready any moment now."

Sylvie ran with her, and they still got a raised eyebrow from Adelaide where she and Lisette laid out the cloth.

"Be careful, Adelaide," said an old man. "Children from far off have strange notions. They can corrupt your child into idle ways."

"Oh, don't be so silly, Ned," called an old woman. "Obviously the girl has to know her way about the valley, and that quickly, or she'll be useless."

Sylvie's face burned. And worse, everyone had to see how pink she was. She sat on the bench and took up the cloth.

"My mother said," said Lisette thoughtfully, "that we should start with handkerchiefs."

"Oh no," said Sylvie. She spread out the cloth. "Yes, handkerchiefs are easier, and simpler. But the court ladies make their own." She looked up. "Or at least have their maids sew them. They put messages in the embroidery or the stitchery."

Lisette giggled. "So that's why the fine ladies had flowers on their handkerchief." She started to tell Marlene about the ladies in waiting with elaborate roses, or thickets of heartsease.

"It must be hard to blow your nose with them," said Marlene.

#

The sun shone on the bench. Snowfall and another kitten, this one with flecks of white in its red tabby coat, sniffed at each other, and Dawn stalked a perilous daisy, while all about them flowers bloomed. Every now and again, someone walking through the village looked at them with undue curiosity, but then walked on.

Sylvie looked at the cloth in her lap. Marlene and Lisette watched in silent interest. They would outdo her in a week, she thought, and picked her words to describe how to do the stitch again. She pushed the needle in. So much harder to show than to stitch.

Lisette tried again. Marlene looked at Sylvie's handiwork. Neither one asked a question, so Sylvie tried to sew again.

"You're geese," spat a girl. Sylvie looked up. The girl looked a little younger than Lisette, her pale brown hair covered, badly, with a green scarf, and she had a basket slung under her arm. "What's the point of all this silliness? The court's going to go. You won't sell it, and all that fancy? What's the point? Sew good enough for use."

"No one's asking you to sew," said Lisette.

"No one's asking you to gather berries," said the other girl, triumphantly. "They sent the princess to protect her, and she wasn't protected."

"So what?" said Marlene.

For a moment, Sylvie froze. Lady Richeza would have chided a sewing girl for saying that. Then she forced out her breath. Lady Richeza was not here. She took a stitch. Neither was Lady Dagmar, who would also have rebuked such speech, but that was because she shouldn't talk like that in court.

They were not in court.

"So what? So what? They'll say there's no purpose to the castle."

"Don't be silly," said Sylvie. All three looked at her. "At many battles, the forces that seemed to hold the field were overwhelmed in the end."

"They hold the castle," said the other girl, sullenly.

"They don't hold the princess," said Sylvie. She stabbed the fabric with the needle. "The castle is useless unless they want to hide the duke in it. Which they would not do because the people of the mountains would not protect him. There is only so much that walls can do."

Then she realized that half a dozen peasants stood about, listening.

One, from the doorway of a cottage, shouted, "They do more than you do, Bessie, standing about gabbing when you should be gathering!"

#

The other girls picked up the skill and sewed on. Faster than she did, Sylvie thought morosely.

A little girl, playing about in the square, abruptly stopped in front of them and said, "Do they tell stories while sewing, in the court?"

Sylvie felt frozen, with all gazes on her.

She found her tongue. "Of course they do," she said. "Sewing for the queen is not that fascinating. So they tell tales, like the one of the old man who was traveling one night when he saw cats having a funeral. Black cats and white cats and red tabby cats and brown tabby cats, all of them yowling, with candles, and a bier and a coffin and all."

That actually did draw every gaze. She thought some of the women spinning on their thresholds faltered. Snowfall walked daintily through the garden, and Sylvie smiled.

"He did not want to go close, but he did not want to offend them, with all their claws to scratch, so he walked slowly along the road and the procession came up to him. They looked at him.

"He was more afraid of them than of wild wolves, he could not run, and one of them said, 'Tell Tom Tiddulum that Tim Tiddulum's dead.'" She spread her hands. "They all started to yowl about Tim Tiddulum's being dead, so he nodded gravely and went on his way to home. Walking—somewhat faster than before."

Marlene and Lisette giggled. Dawn, with a meow, leapt up on the bench and rubbed against Marlene's hand.

"So he told his wife what had happened and asked how he was supposed to tell Tom Tiddulum anything when he had no notion of who Tom Tiddulum was, or where he was, or how to meet him. At that, their black tomcat, sitting on the hearth, lifted his head and said, 'Tim Tiddulum's dead? Then I'm the King of Cats!' and he raced up the chimney—" She threw her hands into the air. "—and they never saw him again!"

Laughter resounded about the village.

The little girl pouted. "I want a *real* story."

"Don't be silly," said Lisette. "She told you a story. And she's not some hired story-teller, she's here to sew."

"You should tell us a story," said Marlene. The little girl ran off. Marlene rolled her eyes and said, "This corner is giving me trouble, Sylvie."

Sylvie went to look at the cloth spread out on her lap.

Across the square, an old woman coughed and coughed. A younger woman came and fussed over her, and she started to complain about the maidens not going to gather the herbs for dyes, that they would start to flower and be useless. And others would go to seed.

Sylvie looked over what Marlene did and went back to sewing. She could sew a great deal before her father could deal with the soldiers.

And, she reminded herself, the more the village looked ordinary, the better her disguise was.

#

"Pssstt—"

Sylvie blinked sleepily. It was dark, and her thoughts fell slowly into place. The morning was even earlier than they usually woke here. The birds chorused in the dark trees, but that was the only sign of approaching dawn, and Marlene stood over her.

"Grab your cloak," she whispered in excitement.

She led Sylvie out the door, with no sign of her parents about, through the village where few people moved at all, and down a misty path with birds calling on either hand. The forest was charcoal gray, the path slippery with dew.

"Be careful," added Marlene, leading her down a dark path between towering oaks. Sylvie rubbed her eyes, and they came out on a cliff. Marlene smiled, more easily seen here than before. "Watch," she whispered.

Sylvie nodded, yawned, and said she would. Looking about revealed no marvels, until she glanced up at the clouds, still dark with night. She gasped.

Marlene followed her gaze, to where the clouds, underneath, were touched with gold, under the still lowering darkness. And she gasped as well. "I've never seen that before!"

They stood and stared.

Then Marlene shook like a horse throwing off a fly. "Look east," she whispered, pointing. "Not just up."

The sky there was grayer than the rest of it. Slowly colors were added to it. Cream and rose and delicate orange as the sun rose, illuminating each mountain and every cloud. The gorge filled with color after color, and slowly the sky grew blue, past dawn, with morning.

And, Sylvie realized, they had to get back to sew more. She started to turn. Then she looked about. Rocks everywhere. Some steep slopes.

"I wonder," said Sylvie, drawing Marlene's gaze. "I wonder if I had to run away to the soldiers, whether I should run here."

Marlene looked startled, and then about. "No. It's a cliff here, and there's no path down. It would not be good."

Sylvie nodded. "A good thing they don't have dogs to hunt me with." They started toward the path. "And Heaven grant that I can run somewhere else—at least not in white!"

When Lisette brought a white gown to embroider that morning, both of them laughed merrily.

#

Mist was melting before day, but the cloth still sat firmly in the basket.

"You can't sit all day every day and sew," said Adelaide, as she put aside the porridge bowls. "You'll give yourselves hunched backs from bending over. You should go berrying today. Lisette will be helping her mother."

Sylvie looked down at her clothes.

"Marlene. show her where the baskets are, and the way."

Sylvie scurried after Marlene. Her heart beat not so much faster as harder, as she wondered how to hide in a berry patch. If she could hide in a berry patch. She bit her lip. At least for long enough. Soldiers would search hard for her.

As the air grew warmer, the path wound about stands of trees and hillocks, until it came out into a sun-lit hollow filled from edge to edge with blackberry brambles. All the bushes were laden with dark berries. A dozen other children and scores of birds already were picking them, but her gaze went about at all the thorns.

"You could hide a castle in here," she said.

A boy laughed. "A castle could hide from you here, but you couldn't get in!"

With many giggles, they talked of sleeping princesses and whether any sleeping prince was ever guarded by thorns, and how it couldn't be because a woman had to get in to watch over him, for three years, three months, three weeks, three days, and three hours, to wake him up.

"And then some other woman slips in the last moment and pretends to be the watcher," said one older girl, sourly.

Then, in a lull, one boy looked at Sylvie. "Are there really black cats in other places?"

"Oh, yes," said Sylvie. "There are black cats, and there are gray cats, and there are brown cats—all sorts of brown. They would think it very strange that here in the mountains you have only white cats and red tabby ones."

The boy's mouth popped open, and he stared at her. And all the children talked more furiously about such a strange thing than about sleeping princes.

Sylvie picked berries.

Chapter 4: The Rain

The morning, a few days later, was dark when Sylvie woke. Darker than it had ever had been in the days—nearly a week—she had been here, except when Marlene had woken her before dawn.

Then she heard the patter of rain.

"Slugabed," called Adelaide, fondly. "It is too dark to sew, all the more in that we do not want your work to get wet." She turned from the fireplace. "But you could learn to spin today."

"Queen Berthe spun," said Sylvie groggily, and pushed back the blankets. The air was cold. She yawned and rubbed her eyes, and could not remember how many days she had been here.

She remembered how many tales she had heard, of how the soldiers hunted for the princess and groused of the cliffs in the mountains, and one tale said that a little girl had told them that the princess had gone into a cottage and then leapt up the chimney and was gone.

Sylvie scuttled over to the hearth, and was glad of the hot porridge. Then, with Adelaide beside her, she sat by the fire, at the spinning wheel, and fumbled with the wool.

Adelaide made it look so easy. *Her* thread was never too thick, or too thin. And it *never* broke.

After a time, when Sylvie had just broken the thread another time, Adelaide took up her knitting and left Sylvie to spin, only glancing over now and again.

The day grew a bit warmer, and its gray a bit paler. Adelaide had Sylvie move over by the window, and let the fire sink. Snowfall prowled out of the shadows and leapt up beside her, to purr against her leg. The rain grew so slight that she could not hear it, but could see the grayness as it fell.

Marlene began to sing under her breath. "Young Jehan was as brave a knight, as ever sailed the seas—"

The knock on the door was faint, but Adelaide rose to open it, greeting Ellen and a gust of cold wet air.

An old woman hobbled in, grumbling of the rain and the cold. Marlene bobbed her head dutifully to age, and Sylvie caught herself and did the same. A peasant lassie should respect her elders.

You did as much for your father's councilors, Sylvie reminded herself.

Ellen grumbled on without a glance at Sylvie, or Marlene, and here was the dye for Adelaide, a disgrace how girls gathered herbs these days, and how in her days, people knew to name their daughters Lena or Ellen, and not Helena.

Sylvie's hand faltered on the wool.

Adelaide quickly asked whether they gathered enough for the orange dye.

The old woman sniffed. "If you'll take third or fourth dip. All those shades of orange from the best to the worst, and they don't even care that it looks just the same as if you didn't bleach the linen right before dyeing it."

Another knock sounded on the door.

"Huh," said Ellen. "What sort of business does anyone have on this dreary day? Driving them out and about?" Her eyes narrowed. "What sort of *honest* business?"

Adelaide opened the door. The newcomer was briefly a dark shadow against the gray, and then he was inside and pushing back his damp hood to show that it was Hendrick.

"Off to see that your work as a knight errant wasn't wasted?" said Ellen.

Hendrick's expression no more moved than a stone would. "Playing the messenger boy."

"Did they—" Adelaide gasped. "Are they coming here? The soldiers?"

Hendrick shook his head, and Sylvie felt relief.

"At least no more than any other place," he amended.

Sylvie winced.

"They seem, thus far, to understand that they need our help—they have no woodsmen in their number, let alone a woodsman who knows these forests and these mountains—"

Ellen harrumphed loudly. "If they are not woodsmen, they will not know how badly they need a guide."

"It is something that can be learned quickly," said Adelaide. "Even by a soldier. They are too many to all get lost in the forest and fall over a cliff."

Ellen muttered something about fools from the lowlands having unbounded ability to disbelieve. "It's a wonder some of the valleys aren't filled up with bones."

"It is folly to assume they are all fools," said Hendrick. "Or that their folly will keep us all safe from them for long enough."

"If they are not fools," said Adelaide, "they are not such fools that they would think that forcing a guide to serve them was a wise move. A guide who could lead them into the deep forest could make use of his knowledge to vanish."

A gust of wind beat at the cottage.

"Perhaps," said Hendrick."They haven't yet roughed anyone up to try to get news. All the more after that child told the tale of the chimney."

They all smiled.

"But they did something with the road to the river. Burned down the bridge, perhaps."

"We'd have seen the smoke!" said Marlene. When everyone looked at her, she blushed.

"We would," said Hendrick."There's also a tale of blocking the pass with a rockfall."

"'less they're all fools" grumbled Ellen, "that's no danger. They've got to get out somehow."

Both Adelaide and Hendrick looked at her, but Ellen seemed to not notice. Sylvie swallowed. The log in the fireplace sighed and settled farther into the coals, and she stared at her hands.

"That will make for hardship," said Adelaide. "There is good reason for the road to go there."

"If they hope they can find the princess," said Hendrick, biting out the words, "they can hope to find another way out. Even a company does not need a road."

"My—" When all their gazes turned to her, she faltered, and forced herself to go on. "My father said that the duke has forces to do things—" She waved a hand."—like that, but that the king does, too."

"It's still harder to get through than to fill it up," said Hendrick, morosely. "*My* father is looking at it. He sent me to talk with the villagers about how to keep safe with the soldiers poking about."

Ellen looked sour. Adelaide looked grave.

Sylvie looked at her sewing. "If—if the king had gotten letters because the princess had written every day, he might have noticed by now."

Marlene looked upset, but Hendrick snorted. Sylvie blinked.

"No matter how regularly the princess wrote," said Hendrick, "messengers could not travel as regularly. If the letters arrived promptly for a time, and then stopped, the king would think that something had happened to the road, or perhaps the river or the messenger, not that something had happened to the princess."

In a brief moment of silence, rain pattered softly on the roof.

Adelaide said."There's going to be a circle tonight. But not until late."

Marlene turned to Sylvie."There's a flower they call ghostweed, and when it blooms in the wood, you stay up until midnight so the witches don't curse you in your sleep."

The rain picked up again, and this time it did not slacken off.

"At least," said Adelaide, "that's the story. Those who stay away seldom seem the worse for it."

"And if it rains like this," said Hendrick, "some people will bide in their cottages and say those who stay up are cursed with folly."

"Will you?" said Marlene.

Hendrick smiled. "Stay away? Oh, no. For tales and songs, I will stay up."

Ellen left. Hendrick talked in a low voice with Adelaide. Sylvie turned back to spinning. Her thread still came lumpy from her fingers. Sylvie tried to tell herself it was tending less so, and caught it only just before it broke. She would have to get them more wool, so they could spin good thread, to replace what she had spun so badly. Her father could do that. She thought.

Adelaide said, in a voice still low, "It has been enough time." She raised it a little and told Sylvie to come over. Marlene looked up, and her mother waved her down. Indeed, she went over to beside Marlene, sat down, and took up her knitting.

Sylvie felt chilled. Silly for a princess to dread crossing a room, she told herself. She stopped the wheel with care and stood up. The gray light from the window dimmed even as she walked over to him and sat in the shadows.

Hendrick hunkered down beside her, and his voice was even lower than when he spoke to Adelaide. "Any courtiers at your castle are prisoners to the soldiers, or traitors to you."

Sylvie swallowed.

"You and you alone might have knowledge of how quickly the king may attack."

"I—"

Hendrick did not speak. A burst of rain pattered on the roof.

She swallowed. "If I remember my lessons rightly, he could take a month to muster his men properly, and a week to arrive. Because if I am captured, and he is alive, my plight, and the kingdom's, is much less than if he is dead."

Hendrick looked grim. "The plight of the mountains may not care. The soldiers are growing desperate. They know if they don't have you when your father arrives, *their* plight is hopeless."

Sylvie swallowed.

"They can't even flee."

"If—" She swallowed again to find her voice. "If someone went to them and offered to show them out of the mountains—" Her voice trailed off. Hendrick looked grim.

"No one would dare. They would take him as a guide to find you." His voice deepened."They haven't beaten anyone yet, but they burned down the hut of an old hermit in the hills. If they burn down too many, people will have nowhere to take refuge. It's not like days of old, where we were few enough to hide in the hills."

Sylvie bit her lip. Her mind felt utterly blank just when she needed to think."Has—has anyone sent a message to my father?" She remembered what Hendrick had said about messengers, and hurried at add, "Could we have gotten news back?"

"Yes, we could have. Because the soldiers know that your father has heard. They talk about it in the woods. It has made them angry and frightened."

Sylvie winced. She hoped she hadn't looked too silly. "If we got him another message—how to find me—"

"We would need some way to show it was really from you."

"Send my dress?"

Hendrick snorted. "That could be a threat that you were prisoner. Or even your murderer feigning that you were still alive. It might be easier to smuggle you out as a message, but they watch every girl they see moving about."

"They have your wardrobe at the castle," said Adelaide. "They could send a score of dresses. Your father does not know what you wore when you fled the castle."

Sylvie swallowed. "I will think of something—of anything I can—to let you get word to my father. And let him know it was I who sent it."

Hendrick's face set like stone. Sylvie swallowed again. She was only a princess, and only a young princess at that. She wondered whether she would be wiser if she had paid more heed to her studies.

"I am sure you will do your best," said Hendrick. He straightened. Sylvie scuttled back over to the spinning wheel, and Adelaide stood. He nodded to Adelaide and left. Adelaide turned from closing the door, murmuring that Hendrick had not always been so grave and serious, he was young to play the Master of the Mountains.

"He is the young master," said Marlene brightly.

Sylvie wished she had looked up the titles in the mountains before she came. Lady Dagmar would have. Lady Richeza—should have. She took up the thread. But then, she was not so little that she could not have done it without being directed. Or work out some things without looking it up. The young master must be the heir.

Sylvie began to spin again. Adelaide came back over to knit. Wind threw rain against the window.

Marlene began to sing, "My mother did me deadly spite, for she sent thieves in the dark of the night."

Chapter 5: The Fire

At times, it seemed that it would rain all day and night, if not forever, damp and dreary and gray, but in the afternoon, the rain lightened. Then, it came and went, but it went more often, and by evening, it stopped. Clouds had not cleared, the grass was still sodden, the path still muddy, and the forest all but glowered.

Adelaide, Otto, and Marlene eagerly took up a brand from the fire. Even Snowfall ran ahead. Sylvie pulled up her skirt and told herself not to be so dainty and—princessly. A peasant girl would be glad of the gathering, and not so fearful of getting mud on her gown.

In the square, a fire blazed. Stools and benches were spread about. People gathered, increasing by the moment. More people than were in the village, thought Sylvie, with more stools and sometimes benches. Many glanced at her and whispered, and feigned they were doing neither.

The fire leapt. Orange light shone over them and cast darker shadows.

She could only hope that their loyalty to the king, or at least Master Gregor, would keep them silent.

Then she told herself that she was a fool. Everyone in the village knew who she was, and their wondering over it would not make them know any better, or worse.

A man pushed out a stool for her to sit on, where the ground was level, and then others for Marlene, and Adelaide, and Otto. Where everyone could see her, of course.

Old women nodded to her, and old men, and little children sometimes ran up to gawk. Adelaide spoke to Otto, and Otto said they would gawk at any stranger.

Sylvie looked down. Snowfall leapt into her lap to purr, and people whispered. Then, Snowfall was a Queen Angelique's kitten. They might stare at her kitten as well as her. She held out her hand, and Snowfall rubbed against it.

One woman walked up to the fire and threw in something. It began to burn, scenting the air with sweetness. And also, Sylvie noted, driving off the night insects before they drew blood.

A gust of wind blew the smoke toward her, and she coughed, like the others around her. Complaints arose—and laughter after a man blamed the gust on the herbs.

Voices chattered on, some talking of the soldiers. One said that the soldiers had come upon a cliff and sworn a great blast, and then slowly trekked around it. A little boy crowed that that was where the cliff had a chimney with a path up, and was shushed with glances at Sylvie.

Sylvie opened her mouth. Then she shut again. Whether she demanded to know because she was the princess, or because she would learn if she were the cousin they called her, they would think her rude.

"Let us have our tales!" said a black-haired man, heartily. "Once upon a time, Queen Genevieve was wed to King Oliver—"

Sylvie blinked and sat up. She had heard of Queen Genevieve and King Oliver. But not much.

"—and was heavy with his child. He went to war, and commended her to the care of his cousin Hugh. But Lord Hugh was angry that King Oliver had married her, and not his daughter Lady Marianna, so when Queen Genevieve gave birth to a beautiful little son, he sent the king a message that she had given birth to a dog. The king was disconcerted, but sent back word to treat her and the dog kindly. Lord Hugh told servants that the king had ordered that she and the boy be put to death. The servants put the baby in her arms, led her out into the forest, and told her to flee to escape Lord Hugh.

"She went through the woods, weeping, calling on Heaven to attest to her innocence, and wondering whether she could live, or they had only sent her to a crueler death, when a white doe appeared before her.

She tried to follow it, and it flitted away, always keeping just in sight, until she came out by a cliff, and it vanished like the morning mist.

"But when she walked a little farther, little white doves flew out from the cliff, and she found the cleft and hid there. The doe returned to give her aid, and there she lived with her son. Until King Oliver returned and found what Lord Hugh had done, and not even the letter Lord Hugh had forged would save him.

"The servants had fled themselves after they had left her in the woods, so King Oliver had no news of where she was. He went hunting to distract himself from his grief. One day, a white doe appeared, and he gave chase. All his huntsmen fell away, and he grew fearful as the doe leapt ravines and thickets, but he gave chase, until the doe disappeared without a trace, and he stood before a cave where the sunlight lay on the grass before it, and his son sported beneath his mother's eye.

"So King Oliver took Queen Genevieve and his son Prince Guillaume back with him, and they lived happily ever after."

"Doves," said a boy. "Pshaw." Others hushed him, and still others argued with them.

"He's right. Doves indeed. In the land of Queen Angelique's cats. A white cat led her to the secret cave."

"Like that one there!" A woman pointed at Sylvie and Snowfall.

"Pshaw," said a man. "The cat saved Sylvie. It does not mean that doves can not save a queen."

Voices rose, with claims about does and doves and cats and kittens. Some children said the boy was King Guillaume, only to be corrected that it was his great-grandfather, before their voices were drowned out in the dispute. Faces turned red, and some of them began to shout. Sylvie looked from face to face. The boy had become King Guillaume, in due course, and then his great-grandson had been named Guillaume, and become king and her father, but no one looked ready to let her speak.

Snowfall sat up and meowed. Sylvie put her arms about the kitten. Adelaide and Otto looked gray, and Hendrick was trying to speak soothingly, but no one listened to him.

There was, for a moment, a lull in the voices.

"I heard," said Sylvie, as loudly as she dared, "that we would tell stories."

People gave her ugly looks.

"I've heard only one. There should be at least two."

A great bear of a man, with a full red beard, started to laugh. It sounded false, but others joined in, and the sound grew more natural.

"Well," snapped one of those quarreling, "you're one of us, to tell stories as well. Tell us a story."

"And not that one about the cat and the chimney," said another.

A third rolled his eyes. "Not again."

There were murmurs of agreement, but Sylvie ignored them as she spoke.

"Once upon a time, when wishing still did some good, there was a freeholder who had a daughter, though his wife had died. One day his widow neighbor told him that his daughter was growing up wild and did not know how to behave. He should marry her and she would bring up his daughter properly, as her own daughter was brought up."

A woman nodded, and there were murmurs of agreement about.

"So they married, and two days after the wedding, her stepmother told her to do all the kitchen work, and went to her father to complain that the girl had learned to be lazy before the wedding, and she would have to punish her for her negligence. He paid no heed to his daughter's complaints, or how ragged and filthy she grew, or how he never saw his wife or her daughter doing any work.

"But before she had worked for a week, one night as she wept by the cold hearth because she had more work than she could do, a cat came to her and told her to be of good heart, trust Heaven, and lie down to sleep. The morning would be better than the evening. She did as the cat said, and in the morning, all her work had been done.

"For a time she managed with the cat's help, but one day, her stepmother saw the cat. She kept watch over the stepdaughter all day and made her do all the work herself, and she was filthy and ragged and weary by the end of the day, and when her father came home, he told her stepmother to give the beggar some coins and send her off.

"That night, the cat said to her, 'Your stepmother is asking your father right now to skin me for a muff, and then she will work you to death. You must take the fine gowns your stepmother has you sew for your stepsister and flee.'

"So she fled, and the cat went with her. It had her go to a castle, where she found a job as a scullery maid, which was not much more pleasant than her father's house. But the cat helped her of a night, and she slept in the corner of the kitchen and ate what they gave her.

"One day, the cat told her to be wakeful and take one of her stepsister's gowns, because the king and queen held a ball, so that their son could choose a bride from the women of the realm. She should dress in the gown and go to the ball, but go away at midnight.

"So she arrived at the ball as lovely as the cloudless dawn, and all the jealous mothers condemned her as a stranger intruding where she had no place, without her mother to escort her, but the prince had no eyes for any maiden there except for her. They danced every dance together, until midnight came."

The people had moved about. They formed a circle about her, to hear clearly. A log in the fire cracked in the silence, and vividly orange sparks formed a plume against the shadows.

Sylvie plunged onward. "But at the cat's command, she left the ball at midnight and went back to the kitchen to work.

"The prince was distraught. He sent soldiers to hunt about the castle, and through the villages nearby. He moped about the castle when they did not find her. But one day, he saw her pouring out water and said that she looked very like the lady at the ball. She said that she was only the scullery maid and ran back to the scullery.

"So he grew cheerful and had his parents hold another ball, and this time to have soldiers circle about the hall to catch that unknown lady. The cat told her to go again, and when midnight came, to run away again. So she did, and the soldiers tried to catch her, and she escaped.

"Then the prince went to a jeweler and had him make him a ring, with a lovely jewel in it. He had his parents hold another ball, and while they danced, he slid the ring on her finger. She ran away at midnight again, and this time the soldiers did not search for her, but when she went back to the kitchen, the ring was so lovely that she turned the stone into her palm rather than take the ring off.

"The next day the prince had her bring him a dish, and saw the ring, and caught her hand, and said this was the woman he wished to marry. And they did, and they made the cat a margrave and let it live by the fire and never chase mice unless it wished to, and they lived happily ever after."

Silence reigned. A log in the fire settled deeper into the coals with a sigh. After a moment, people glanced at each other, and then Marlene hopped to her feet.

"Young Jehan was as brave a knight, as ever sailed the seas—"

This time she sang it through to the end, and others took up tales, and there was chatter in between, and about, and Hendrick moved among them. He looked very grave, like a royal official among courtiers, and someone wondered whether the duke would be a danger.

"Yes," said Sylvie. "Yes, he would. He has a duchy by the ocean, and he says that the mountains are a bother, and they deserve to have all the outlaws and murderers and brigands go there."

The men and women about her looked at her with doubt, and she said, "That is why he is having so much trouble searching. No one who knows the forest or mountains is in his service."

"That would hinder them," said a spry, white-haired woman. "Indeed, you might learn enough woodcraft to outwit them yourself. If you went into the woods."

"That may not be wise," said Hendrick.

The woman rolled her eyes. "And you are so wise, yourself, young Hendrick? Will another doe came from the forest to lead her?"

"There's *Snowfall*," said Marlene.

"Who led her to Master Hendrick to guide her," said the woman. "One should not put the Lord your God to the test. Sylvie should learn the forest herself. And gathering herbs is as good a guise as any."

"Not alone," said Adelaide, firmly. "And not tomorrow."

"The day after will do," the woman conceded.

Chapter 6: The Forest

Sylvie yawned and rubbed her eyes. Dozens upon dozens of stars still shone in the sky. Villagers already moved about, by the dozen, all awake and with their wits about them.

Marlene yawned, and Sylvie felt a little less foolish.

Marlene looked about. "Were there servants that didn't get up this early at the castle?" she said, in a low voice.

"Some," said Sylvie. Her breath was white on the air. She pulled the cloak closer. "When the courtiers danced until midnight, someone had to clean up after them. At least well enough to manage the next day. Then they slept. But even then, other servants would be up by now."

Marlene looked startled as that number of servants, but then ran off. Sylvie looked after, and then hurried to join her as she ran toward Yvona. Even though Adelaide had not thought to tell her the woman's name until tucking her into bed last night.

Yvona glanced at them and raised an eyebrow looking at their baskets. "They'll do," she said. "Though it's a good thing you are coming to learn woodcraft and not gather for market."

"I don't think we could learn the tricks quickly enough," said Sylvie. She looked at her basket. "Not unless you took us to a *big* patch, and it was easy to gather, and we gathered all day."

Yvona smiled. "Not even then, I think. You would never gather enough to sell a batch to the merchants who come up the road. Much better to sell them to the man who'll sit by the wayside to buy and then sell them all together." She frowned. "You do have a nuncheon?"

"Bread and cheese," said Marlene.

"And water to drink," said Sylvie. "She had us eat a big bowl of porridge this morning."

Yvona's smile deepened. She nodded and walked toward the woods. And not the road at all, Sylvie noted.

"Isn't the road blocked?" said Marlene, walking along. "For selling?"

"Why, haven't you heard?" Yvona gave them a sideways glance. "The soldiers did, indeed, try to block the road. Chopping down trees over it. They tried to roll down boulders, but one of them died when a boulder rolled the wrong way."

"So they blocked the road with trees?" said Sylvie. If they chopped the trees up, they would have wood and the road would lie open.

"They got one to land on the road. Mostly its branches. And then two of them died when a tree landed wrong."

"The branches are trouble," said Marlene. "If someone has a cart."

"That will not last long." Yvona shook her head. "It's not like there were an earthquake, or the duke sent a wizard to fill it in. If he wants to claim the kingdom, he will have to claim the mountains too."

"He does not care about the mountains. He says they spend too much there." Sylvie looked at her basket. "For herbs. He says they are too costly and they don't need them and they should spend their money in their own duchy."

Yvona's smile deepened. "Some of them are worth it. If he becomes king, he will learn what are the limits of his power. Follow me."

She did not go by a path, not even to leave the village. They pushed through the thicket brush by the wayside, holding back branches for each other, until they reached inside. The spreading branches and their leaves hid the sky above and darkened all below, and they walked on the dead leaves. Thickets of bushes, and stands of bracken, vividly green, complicated their way. The low growing moss and plants at least could be walked on.

Yvona glanced at them now and again but said nothing. Perhaps she was trying to learn how well they could watch. When Sylvie pointed out the low-growing yellow flower with six petals, and each of its leaves six fronds, Yvona smiled and said it was pretty, but not serviceable.

"It can be dried to freshen your clothes in their chest during the winter, but in truth, there are better herbs for that." She glanced at Sylvie. "They might sell it to courtiers, to spare the better herbs."

Sylvie nodded solemnly. Then she remembered that the woodcraft was more important. "Do they always grow here? So they mark the way?"

Yvona said, "The yellow stars grow wherever they please, and places generally do please them. They do not mark the way. Few herbs are useful that way. I will tell you when we find such a patch."

Sylvie nodded, solemnly, and then a fiery red bird flitted through the woods. When it caught the sunlight, she started. It glowed there, so red and orange that it looked as if there should be smoke as well.

Yvona laughed. "Those are our firebirds. You hear the most fantastic tales about them."

"Do people try to catch them?" said Sylvie, looking up at her.

"Not often," said Yvona. "They don't even often come to try."

"The firebird must not go and eat up all the grain in the fields, or steal all golden apples from trees," said Sylvie reflectively, and Marlene laughed.

Their nests would not be a good signpost, either, thought Sylvie. A firebird's, or any other bird's from a hawk to a warbler. She had not seen any nests, for one.

She watched as they walked, for other things she could mark the way with. The trees and the brush and the ferns looked as featureless as a lawn. They held no nests that she could see. Odd trees, twisted or lopsided, stood here and there, and sometimes she saw boulders. She tried to remember them. A stream was more useful, she realized, because it could only run one way. It fell over stones in tiny cascades, and pooled, and ran along where the banks gave it an easy path.

She blinked at the white. It could not fall hard enough to make it foam—

"Look at that," said Sylvie, and pointed to tiny milk-white flowers, growing in the mud against a stone. Their blossom hung over their dark green leaves.

"Ah, the moonlight," said Yvona. "One name, others call them pearl flowers. You were sharp-eyed to see it, but we will not gather it." She hesitated. "It would be lying to tell you that we never gather it, but its use is very rare. It can be used as a purgative, at need, but it is dangerous because it takes very little to give too much and poison the patient."

Both girls stared at her.

"It is the dose that makes the poison," she said, with complete conviction. "That is why a herbwoman must study for years to administer some herbs. Why, some can be given only distilled, because plant differs from plant in splendor, and dosage. Neither of you have time to learn that in a season. Mastery takes years."

Sylvie fell silent. She hoped her time here would be short. She wondered what the duke would do to keep her in hiding for any long time. She might have to run away to become a scullery maid in another kingdom for safety.

Yvona brought them downstream, to where stones sprawled. Their shoes squished in the mud but the stones were close enough for stepping stones, and they soon stood on dry ground again.

Sylvie thought how it looked very like that stream that Hendrick and she had followed. It was not a good way-sign.

She sighed and looked ahead.

"Looking for a way to return?" said Yvona.

Sylvie said, brightly, "Looking to learn what I can. I might use it to run away. Then I wouldn't return."

"There aren't many places to go if you flee," said Yvona. "They don't even bring up more cattle in the summertime, since they have no pastures for them."

"Running away from soldiers would be better than staying put," said Sylvie. "Maybe the legends are right, and Snowfall could hide me. Like Queen Genevieve."

Yvona looked at her and raised an eyebrow. "You wouldn't wait for a white doe?"

"Snowfall's a white kitten," said Marlene. "Maybe it's the same."

They came over a hill, and in a hollow, low-growing flowers bloomed in pale blue. From one side to the other, utterly filled. It showed more blue than green, the pale blue of the sky, and the sky near the horizon.

Sylvie's breath gushed out. It took her a minute even to think that this hollow was smaller than the blackberry patch. The tree boughs were so thick overhead that sunlight formed only splatters here. Once she collected herself, she saw how bluish the leaves were. They were only barely green.

"The secret of the skydrops," said Yvona, "is that their early leaves can be used to make blue dye. Not the full growth, and not the petals. The early, green ones."

Sylvie looked away. "So, this is too late."

"Much too late," said Marlene. "They brought them into the village—" She frowned. "—when we hadn't even heard that the princess was coming. Just after Easter."

"The princess didn't even know she was coming, then," said Sylvie, and she and Marlene glanced at each other and smiled in the shade.

Yvona laughed a little and walked about the edge of the flowers. The undergrowth was a bit thicker here.

"Children," she said. "Take care to not tread on the skydrops. Otherwise they will not be here to make dye for the princess. Once she learns of them, and it's their harvest time again."

Sylvie nodded solemnly, and they scrambled after the herbwoman. It was harder than it looked, clambering over roots and rocks and through the greenery without stepping down into the patch. The slope, thought Sylvie, didn't help. It was like walking on the edge of a bowl.

They reached the top of a hillock, and the ground was flat. Or flatter. Sylvie looked ahead, to see if the sky could be seen through the trees ahead. It couldn't, but there was a glimpse of dazzling whiteness, darting among trees, ahead of her.

"Snowfall!"

She barely realized that she had brushed by Yvona, running toward the kitten. Snowfall took a few steps toward her, and she swept the kitten up and kissed her, turning as she went. With Snowfall in her arms, she blinked. The ground was thick with brambles and ferns. She pulled a leaf out of her hair, and Snowfall purred.

Yvona gaped as if the kitten were actually a fall of snow. Then she plugged toward them and started to scold Sylvie, without being very clear about Sylvie's fault. Except that she didn't think that a kitten had any place gathering herbs.

"But it's one of Queen Angelique's kittens!" said Marlene.

Yvona stood in the ferns and had a stubborn look on her face, like a grown-up who didn't even mean to try to be fair. Sylvie scrambled back. Snowfall purred and did not struggle. Which was more reasonable than Yvona.

"Snowfall got me out of the castle in time when the duke's men came."

Yvona looked at her with narrowed eyes.

"Maybe Snowfall is heavenly aid," said Sylvie. "It would be wrong to demand that Heaven send an angel rather than a white doe, or a white cat."

Yvona looked down at Snowfall. Snowfall purred.

Yvona rolled her eyes. "Don't let it sleep in your basket. Or it will sleep on the herbs. And crush them." She turned to the slope. Then she looked back to Sylvie, and her voice was ominous. "And it's a good thing you caught it here. Keep that kitten close as we go over the hill."

Sylvie flinched. Marlene pulled closer to her, and they walked slowly up the slope. At the top, Yvona stopped. The forest before them looked much like the forest behind them, except in one place, a stand of flowers stood with white blooms in great white puffs.

The flowers didn't glow, Sylvie thought. She was almost certain that they did not glow.

"Ghostweed," said Yvona, flatly. "It is not just an excuse to stay up late and tell tales. You have to be wary of it. When someone, or something, walks through it, its seeds float off. Even when the wind goes through it. And the floating seed is dangerous. You don't have a white doe to lead you away. And your kitten—" She glanced over to where Snowfall purred away.

Sylvie swallowed. "We have you, to lead us away."

Yvona snorted. "You should not listen to too many troubadours' tales about how the lady, fair of face, is protected from all harm."

"She is pretty," said Marlene. "Hendrick said so, and everyone else agreed with him."

"The duke doesn't care," said Yvona sourly. "Actual princesses don't have to be fair of face. Just be princesses."

"And hide. And learn about herbs and things. That's *statecraft*." Sylvie twirled about. "Becoming a scullery maid would be easier. I had to learn about it so I could oversee the kitchens."

Yvona almost smiled.

"But if we can't gather the skydrops, or the ghostweed, and don't want to gather the moonlight, there must be something else you are looking for," said Sylvie. "You wouldn't gad about just to show silly girls about the forest."

"Over here," said Yvona, "we will find our roots. And you twain will start to learn the art of simpling. You do not know how to simple until you have learned every profitable plant, how and when to gather them, what to gather, and how to tell them from useless plants or worse, dangerous ones."

Sylvie bobbed her head and looked with Marlene where Yvona pointed. Low, dark green, with oval leaves.

"You can see that they are not in bloom. They are never in bloom. Green janes, we call 'em." And Yvona began the lecture on their leaves, pointing out that they came in pairs on opposite sides, and each pair and the one above it formed a cross in how they pointed. Sylvie listened. And dug. And carefully buried broken-off bits of root—to regrow—as Yvona directed, and nodded solemnly when Yvona explained that no one dug them before Midsummer.

"Time was when a lass might dig if she really needed the money. Not now. The herb-buyers, they know if they buy it before, they will find no one with the herb soon after."

They tamped down the dirt as carefully as if they were planting a rose bush in the royal garden and went on along the hill.

The day wound on. Many hours were spent learning how to move among the bracken and brush without tearing her clothes to shreds, how to tell where they could safely climb hills without breaking their bones, and when they should go around, how to measure whether a rock would bear her weight without twisting her ankle. The labor sometimes had Sylvie, and Marlene, yawning.

Then they would find plants. She listened to accounts of the leaves and flowers recounted with the intensity of a tale of wars between two kingdoms that her father was treating with.

Then they walked again, between the plants, up hill and down, past boulders and under cliff-faces, or over them.

When they walked in silence, she thought of the herbiary in her father's castle. Easier to gather from, but she thought Yvona showed her more plants in a single day than the herbiary ever grew.

Near noon, Yvona had them sit on a boulder, gray and lichen-covered, in a stand of maple and beech. There, they ate and watched the sunlight flecks dance on the forest floor from the breezes. Sylvie wondered a little whether it was before or after noon, but then, it was uncommonly hard to judge with the forest. She took the last bite, and swallowed it.

"Knights," said Sylvie as she knocked away crumbs, "talk of how hard it is to climb mountains. And how winded they are at the top."

Yvona lifted an eyebrow and stood. "Who would want to climb to the top of a mountain? It's only in tales that some wondrous flower grows there."

"Beacons," said Sylvie slowly. "Also, you can see over the land better."

Yvona snorted. "That must work better when there are no trees."

"Oh yes," said Sylvie, scrambling up. "Much better."

"Much, much, much better," said Marlene dreamily, and they both giggled. Then they followed after Yvona for more simpling.

After a couple more hours, Sylvie stood on an outcropping and stretched. They were near another cliff-face—the tallest yet—and the thick tree canopy hid the sky entirely from sight. In the thick shadows, Sylvie saw the color, a flash in the woods. She gasped. For a moment, the dull red, like dried blood, did not take shape, and her thoughts flew to a magical deer, and how it would be wiser to flee this one.

Marlene looked over and paled. Both of them skittered closer to Yvona, where she gathered a herb too delicate for them to touch.

"We have to flee," said Sylvie.

"The soldiers are here," said Marlene. She glanced back.

"We can't see them here so we have a chance," said Sylvie. "All the more in that—we aren't in red." She waved at the brown skirts. "Or white."

Yvona looked pale. She pitched her voice softer than many whispers. "That helps less than you might think." She did not look at them, but about. "Have care. Ghostweed grows about here, and we might have to be silent near it—so silent I can not warn you again."

Snowfall meowed. And leapt from Sylvie's arm. Sylvie's hands flew up in surprise, but Snowfall was already darting under ferns before she thought to snatch. Yvona looked ready to shout at the kitten. Was Snowfall going *toward* the soldiers? Sylvie scrambled after.

No sooner than she moved than Snowfall darted onward, with no more difficulty than if the overgrown forest floor were a road broad enough for an army. White flashed among the ferns' green. Enough to follow. Sylvie gave the kitten a narrowed gaze. As if it were intentionally leading her. Toward a cliff.

"I think there's a chimney up here," said Marlene, softly.

"What folly are you two children up to?" said Yvona. "What if you found a bear with her cubs here?"

Sylvie scrambled on. Marlene was right. The cliff did hold a narrow cleft. No bear could fit in it. But the rock was rough and offered handholds, and footholds, if she put her attention to it. Ferns and mosses grew only here and there. She frowned. Shadows made it hard to see the way.

Snowfall was a pale glimpse, ahead of her, higher up the cleft.

Yvona's voice was sour. "You do know that you can only climb a chimney in a cliff by putting your back to one side of it?"

"Then this must not be a chimney," said Sylvie. "Only a cleft." She inched forward and started to climb. A cave might shelter them. If it would not be so pleasant as Otto and Adelaide's cottage, it would be harder for the soldiers to find.

"Bring your basket," said Yvona sharply.

Startled, Sylvie looked down. A down-cast Marlene was putting her basket back on her arm.

"No matter that it's harder to climb with it. They find it, then they know that you were here, and that you fled," said Yvona, ominously. "They will not *care* whether you are with the princess."

Sylvie swallowed and looked at her own basket. Snowfall meowed, and she looked back to the path. White or not, Snowfall was hidden entirely by the ferns ahead. She climbed after, and it was trickier than it looked. Sometimes her back brushed against rock as she reached for a new handhold, and sometimes she thought that helped keep her from falling. Sometimes she had to circle about rocks and ferns that Snowfall could easily slip through.

When she climbed one steep slab, she found before her nose a shelf of rock. Flat as a floor, not tall enough to stand up in, but they could all sit.

Snowfall already sat there.

She crawled out on it. For the thickness of the ferns and the trees, she could not see the forest floor. Perhaps anyone who stood on the forest floor could not see her.

In the shadow of the cliff, Snowfall started to lick her paw.

Marlene climbed up beside her and looked at the way up.

"We can't outrun them," said Sylvie. She pulled up her knees and put her arms about them. "We have to hide."

Yvona, clambering up after them, nodded at that. "Draw back. Into the shadows. Give the soldiers no chance to see."

A shout over their heads made Marlene grimace and crawl back.

It was awkward with the rocks about, only Snowfall fit easily, and Yvona grumbled that it was all very well for youngsters, but her old bones needed more respect. Then she told them to shift about.

Minutes later, they all huddled in the stone. Yvona muttered something under her breath about learning to hide at her age, but then fell as silent as the stone. Marlene and Sylvie tried to imitate her. Sylvie wondered if her harsh breathing, from climbing, echoed.

She opened her mouth and then, quickly, shut it again. Maybe her breathing would pass as breeze.

A bird began to sing. Sylvie's head bent. She already started to feel stiff, and they would sit here in silence as long as the soldiers searched. At that, the soldiers would not be driven off by a search party looking for her—either of her father's men, who were not near enough, or of the mountain folk, who were not enough to risk the danger.

The risk to her, too. Fighting the soldiers would only make them suspect that she was near and needed defense.

So they would search as long as they searched.

Shouts echoed, every now and again. The anger in them helped her keep still, but it felt so very odd to have Marlene and Yvona there and be unable to speak. Even Snowfall seemed to realize the gravity. The kitten did not purr.

Moments inched on. Sylvie wished that they had not eaten all their food and shifted back a little, against the cliff. At least they had water.

Instantly her mouth felt dry as a drought. And a shout resounded down the cleft. The soldier must be all but on top of it. She did not dare speak.

The sunlight still glittered between the leaves, sometimes dazzling, but even here, Sylvie could see it grew, slowly, more golden and orange. She bit her lip. Evening could only hinder the soldiers. It was easier to hide with more shadows. Still more if the soldiers heard the tales about the mountains and decided to flee ghosts and bogies and witches.

It would be cold at night, and they would go hungry. She swallowed.

The soldiers' shouts came clear now and again. Sometimes expressing revulsion at the forest. Sometimes reminders that some forest sprite had killed Tom and Hans and Wat when they tried to block the road. Sometimes angry at how hard the search was, and cursing Lady Richeza for her folly and sloth. Sometimes fierce reminders that the duke could be more dangerous than an ogre.

That reminder was enough to keep Sylvie still despite the growing dark and coolness. But then it occurred to her that it would be hard to drink in the shadows. She pulled out her water bottle and showed it to Yvona. Who nodded.

She gulped down the water gratefully, and Marlene drank her own within minutes. The sky was visible enough that she could see some pink and orange in the west, but among the trees, it grew dark.

Sudden shouts of eagerness were followed by the sound of soldiers running. Marlene and Yvona both looked as consumed with hope as she was. Then she realized. Some of them were shouting about seeing white.

She leaned forward to whisper into Marlene's ear, "They're running where the ghostweed is."

Marlene's face lit up. Yvona's face darkened, and Marlene whispered to her. Yvona looked even more grim and gestured both of them to come close.

Her voice was low but grave. "That may help. It may also enrage them."

Marlene cringed. Sylvie nodded and leaned against the wall. A princess could not show how frightened she was. She swallowed and told herself that even if the ghostweed infuriated them, it might also help.

"Give me your baskets," said Yvona. Sylvie blinked and obeyed. Yvona fit them all together, and pushed them into the back-most corner, hidden by shadow.

Where, Sylvie slowly realized, the baskets could neither encumber nor betray them. The soldiers could not find the baskets and realize that three had been here, but the baskets would not weigh the three of them down if they could flee. She bit her lip. Could they flee? Ever? The soldiers still moved, but they converged below the cliff.

Where the ghostweed was, and they still talked of white. Perhaps they gathered force for their folly.

Moments inched by, and her heart pounded. This was slower than all the hours of tedious waiting.

The soldiers' calls to each other were broken by shouts of rage. Within moments, white flecks like snow drifted on the air.

Yvona's voice was low but definite. "If *that* drifts in here, put your sleeve over your mouth and nose. To protect yourself."

Sylvie bit her lip. The ghostweed patch—the more she thought on how far it was, the more frightened she was. The soldiers had to be an absolute fury. They might not even take *her* alive.

Out of the corner of her eye, she saw white. She looked over, ready to warn the others about the ghostweed flecks.

Snowfall slept on the stone.

Sylvie closed her eyes, envying her own kitten, and tried to judge from the shouts. They sounded as if they were regrouping. Then she heard a rustle, close by.

Her eyes flew open. Something in green and brown moved through the cleft, coming down from above. Something human—her heart hammered—something in green and brown—and she could not make out a face—

Snowfall meowed.

The figure stopped. The head moved. A hood like a mask covered it entirely, with two dark gaps where eyes were. Sylvie fought down a shriek.

Then hands went up to move aside a mask of green and brown, and show that it was Hendrick.

Sylvie's breath gushed out. She managed to keep from standing but waved. Her hand looked very pale in the gloom.

"Make haste," said Hendrick. "We can smuggle you away while they curse the ghostweed." He glanced at Yvona. "They sent me down because they were not sure it was wide enough for a man, but I got through. I think you all can climb."

Yvona snorted. "I think the chance is good enough to take."

Snowfall already scurried ahead, past Hendrick. Sylvie inched forward and bit her lip again. She was so stiff.

"It's a fair step here," said Hendrick. "Let me help you."

He hefted her up, and she had to fumble for the handhold. The sunset cast more shadows than light, and nothing was distinct. It was a sorry and laborious business, with the cleft narrower and steeper than below, ferns growing in inconvenient places, and everything being muffled in gloom. Increasing gloom, until her hand fumbled about and found a root, and she did not quite know what to do.

A man's hands came down to catch her about the waist. Then he lifted her up, on the forest floor, and back away from the cliff. She blinked, looking about. Through the tree branches, a star could be seen. Other shadowy figures came out of the trees, and three up from the cleft.

In the last of the sunlight, Hendrick put a finger to his mouth. Snowfall emerged, the brightest thing in the forest, and looked up at Hendrick. He looked down, and then picked the kitten up. As softly as he could, he said, "Haste is still needed."

Yvona nodded, and Sylvie found herself swept up by the man who had helped her from the cleft, and slung over his shoulders like a roll of far-fetched fabric borne off a ship. He strode through the woods among the other men, down hollows and up rises, letting her hands brush against shrubs, before she realized that Marlene had also been slung over a man's shoulders. She waved. Marlene waved back.

Yvona scrambled to keep up but did not complain.

The moon rose, adding little light to the way with the thickness of the leaves. Every now and again, it rose a little higher, the only way she had to mark time.

The moon had risen, but none too high, when their path descended a slope. Sylvie thought that Yvona had not even brought them near this place. Steep slopes rose to either side, and turned. These hills blocked out much of the moonlight that the trees let through, but the men stopped in a hollow, with sides steep and hard to climb, and no visible path out.

Not even the one they had come on. Sylvie swallowed.

Low voices among the trees spoke of "your father" and how lucky it had been they had caught Hendrick when the news came, that they had found the princess only because they followed the soldiers, and as the man lowered her—and the other man, Marlene—to the ground, one man broke off, into the woods. Sylvie scowled. She could not tell whether he went up the way they had come down. A messenger to tell Hendrick's father?

Then someone else came up to her. Even the gloom, Hendrick looked slighter than the men about him. He held out Snowfall, the white fur barely visible, and Sylvie took the kitten into her arms. Snowfall snuggled against her.

"It's safe enough to speak, if we do so quietly, but we can not have light." He glanced up at the lacy leaves that did not entirely hide the sky.

Sylvie nodded, blushed a little, and said, "I understand," before telling what had happened. Marlene and Yvona came up, but did not contradict her, or add to anything she said. Hendrick listened in silence. She thought the other men did, as well, but then, they might need to know.

Hendrick ran a hand through his hair. The evening was too dark to see his face, but he sounded like he was scowling. "The soldiers were too obvious moving from the castle. We do not know how they found their way here."

"They were not searching until they were nearly upon you, Your Highness," said a man, heavily.

"How long will we have to stay here?" said Yvona, louder than Sylvie thought wise.

"As long as it takes," said another man, his voice deep and stern. "For now, take your rest. We have food. And water."

"We drank water on the ledge," said Marlene. "*Sylvie* insisted."

The man hesitated. "Everyone knows she's the princess."

Marlene put her hands on her hips. "The soldiers don't. So don't fall into bad habits."

"Come drink more water, Marlene," said Yvona. "And you, too, Sylvie."

Chapter 7: The Court

It felt like court, with the trees towering about them like the castle's pillars.

Their seat—hers and Marlene's and Yvona's—was a boulder, but the men spread blankets on it. It was not cold, or as hard as the ledge had been, and Snowfall curled up and slept, though Sylvie wondered how.

They ate. People hurried about them, doing this and that and talking in low voices like courtiers, down to not telling her what they were doing.

Sylvie licked her fingers. It was darker than court. Even in the summer, when no one lit candles for the heat, and everyone went as far into the castle as they could for coolness, it was not so dark as this in the shadows. She had heard the man who brought them food called Karel, but she could not recognize him among the figures.

She doubted that she would recognize him by daylight. If he spoke, perhaps.

Voices broke out in excited babble. Moments later, others spoke in tones of sharp rebuke. And then subsided. Sylvie leaned forward as if she could hear more clearly that way.

It took a minute before it was clear that scouts had returned, bearing the news that the soldiers had taken off back to the castle, swearing that the woods were bewitched.

Torches began to flare. Light gleamed over the clearing and the scores who gathered there. Sylvie breathed a sigh of relief. They must really believe the soldiers gone. The company slowly became clear.

When they wanted to rescue a princess, thought Sylvie, they did it quite handsomely. Torchlight danced over the clearing in black and orange. Her gaze moved from face to face, as she tried to remember any of them. She could guess that some of them were not Karel, because they lacked his height and build.

"Is that Dennis?" whispered Marlene.

Sylvie glanced over. It did look like him, though she had not seen enough of him in the village to be sure. Voices drifted over. They spoke with ugly tones.

Hendrick spoke, clearly, loudly. "They did not go to the village. They came looking for someone gathering herbs. Not sending her back to the village would draw more attention than doing so. Just do not send her out again."

Yvona shuddered. "It will be a few days before I go out myself," she muttered.

People began to move. Sylvie carefully ate and drank the last of the bread and water. Snowfall showed no sign of stirring. For a moment, Sylvie looked about, but no one carried a basket. They had not, after, tried to gather herbs but a princess.

She stood and picked up Snowfall as Yvona and Marlene scrambled up.

The torches started to form a line, and she took a step toward it. Hendrick steered them into a place, and they walked out of the hollow by a different path, narrower than the one they had gone in by. Fortunately, not steeper, but enough to remind her that carrying Snowfall in a basket would have been easier. Step by step by step, they went on.

At the height, to her relief, the way grew wider, and they walked down a gentle slope.

At every cross path, it seemed, men turned off to their own homes and bore their torches with them. Each time, they walked on in less light.

Enough to see her footing. Enough to see how tired Marlene looked. And how bone-weary Hendrick looked.

She found herself yawning. She had thought she would be glad to not be carried. Blearily, she tried to peer through the trees.

The torchlight was echoed by lights ahead, and Sylvie blinked. Moments later, shouts sounded, and she realized that the village stood there. She staggered, and Hendrick grabbed her arm.

Moments later, Adelaide was upon them, her arms about Sylvie and Marlene, weeping about their danger and their safety and the marvel of their return, and pressing them so close that the cloth kept them blind, and Snowfall sprang free.

"They're both fine," said Hendrick, and yawned.

"We have heard nothing of substance all day," said Otto, his voice deep. Sylvie looked up to see him cradling Snowfall.

Marlene rubbed her eyes.

"They are fine," said Adelaide, reluctantly releasing them. "What else matters?"

"We went with Yvona," said Sylvie. "Soldiers came. We hid. They blundered into ghostweed, and we got away." Then she yawned again. "Snowfall got us away, then Hendrick got us away."

"We can tell you in the morning," mumbled Marlene.

Snowfall merowed.

"You slept," said Marlene, accusingly, to the kitten.

"Bed, for both of you," said Otto.

#

Snowfall purred. Sylvie opened her eyes. Marlene was also stirring. Sunlight slanted through the window to the floor, and Sylvie started and sat up. It was *so* late—

She scrambled from bed. What was she supposed to be doing? She should remember it from last night. Marlene yawned, and looked appalled at the hour. Snowfall, on the floor, stirred, and voices sounded outside.

One said, clearly enough, "Dennis, you're drunk."

"It's madness," said Dennis, weakly. "With all these soldiers!"

Sylvie blinked, and remembered. Marlene sat up, but looked thoughtful. After all, even if Adelaide had told them what they were to do today, they might not have to do it, or even should not do it.

Sylvie straightened out her clothes, and Marlene joined her.

"Yes, we will have to see about them," said Hendrick, his voice clear.

Dennis harumphed. Sylvie and Marlene edged over to the door. The sunlight fell on them, but Dennis's attention did not leave Hendrick. Half a dozen men surrounded them both.

Adelaide quietly came over to the girls.

"They said," said Dennis scornfully, if unsteadily, "that you called her pretty."

"She is, as befits a princess," said Hendrick. "You should have seen her in the fir grove, with sunlight shining about her, glowing in her white and blue gown and fair hair against the gloom about her." He waved his hand. "True, she lacks the stately, queenly, regal beauty, but she will grow into it in time, no doubt. For now, she is as lovely as a birch grove with the sun shining through the green leaves, and her laughter is as sparkling as a running brook."

Sylvie thought she would turn scarlet, her face heated so.

Hendrick spread his hands. "And from this, you learn it is unwise to let your son read through books of poetry. He may learn to gabble like some courtier at court."

Laughter resounded. Sylvie's breath came out in a gush. No one talked of her like that at court. Probably because they did not think they could gain by it. They would talk to her father like that. More to her mother. Some to the great nobles who, they assumed, had influence.

The duke had heard much talk in that vein.

Another man clapped Dennis on the back and talked of a hedge that needed work before the sheep got out and ate all the barley.

"Or the barley got in and ate all the sheep!" said a bright-eyed boy, and everyone laughed.

Hendrick pulled back, toward the cottage, and saw the two of them. His face brightened as he came back into the shadow. "And to think that a messenger already came because my mother insisted they must have news you arrived safely."

Adelaide smiled. "So she did. Sleepy, but safely."

"Consider all the dreadful perils that could befall her in these hills," said Hendrick. "No wonder my mother wondered."

"Didn't you send a messenger?" said Marlene. "That you would see us safe here, and stay the night?"

Sylvie blinked, and then eyed Hendrick. He didn't look tired.

He nodded. "Just think of what my mother would think if I walked home after seeing you safely here."

Marlene laughed. Sylvie felt solemn. She was her father's only child and the heir to the throne. Hendrick was his father's only child and the young Master of the Mountains.

More slowly, Hendrick said, "And my father insists that you come to the manor court. There is talk about the mountains. Troubling talk."

Sylvie blinked again. Had he decided that since getting the news about the soldiers?

Snowfall meowed.

"And not just the tale with the chimney."

Sylvie felt cold. What would bringing her to the manor court do? If her father had had her brought to court in session—she would go to find out as well as to obey her father.

She straightened, glanced up at Adelaide, and managed to find her tongue. "You have to talk to Otto and Adelaide about that."

Hendrick nodded. "I can wait. After so long roving over the hills, and getting woken so early by the messenger, it will be a welcome rest."

Marlene yawned, and said, "I'll go find Father."

Sylvie stood where she was and felt awkward. Her hands moved about, as if seeking work. Then she said, "I'll get my sewing. So I will look like a peasant girl."

Gravely, Hendrick nodded. Sylvie felt even more awkward. She turned and went inside. The sewing was over here, and Adelaide had put it away carefully since she and Marlene were to go out gamboling over the hills. She opened the wicker case with care, and heard a meow. Dawn came to poke an orange nose in, and she warded off the kitten while fishing for cloth as neatly as she could. There was, indeed, work that could be done, she concluded, and heard Adelaide, and Otto as well, talking outside.

With cloth in hand, she emerged back into the day, with Dawn trotting after.

Otto scowled in thought, while Adelaide remonstrated. "Taking her over the hills after all that happened? We already know that the soldiers were looking for her where she was."

"This village is closer to that place than my father's hall is," said Hendrick. "The soldiers could find her here, if they return."

Otto snorted. "If."

"They were—quite fervent about liars as they left." Hendrick hesitated. "My father has sent men to find out, as carefully as they can, whether anyone shared Richeza's fate."

Sylvie looked at the sewing in her hand and felt cold.

"She can't go alone," said Adelaide. "An escort is not enough, it would not be proper. I must go. And we will take Marlene as well. A princess should have a companion if I must step away."

"She will need an escort as well," said Otto. "I will go."

Sylvie swallowed.

"My father will send men," said Hendrick. "As for me and my men, we will stay. At least no one can then claim she was left unguarded. The men can keep watch on the ways."

Otto nodded and talked with him, both in low voices. Sylvie eyed them and edged up to Adelaide to whisper.

Adelaide smiled at the sewing in her hands. After a bite to eat, she and Marlene settled before the cottage and mended. Good, practical peasant sewing. The village moved about them, but Hendrick left and reappeared with his sword. He sat and inspected his blade as soberly as any guard at her father's castle.

Sylvie said, dreamily, "We would sit about a garden at court. We would sew. If nothing so practical as this."

"That would be for the maids," said Marlene, confidently.

"That would depend on how grand you were," said Sylvie.

Marlene blinked and stared.

"And whether your governess thought you needed to work on your stitches."

Marlene giggled.

"But even if you needed to do all your plain work, when you were in the garden, where others could see, you did fancy work. Gentlemen would come and talk, or tell stories, or sing. It would be the gentlemen who would bring a lute or a pipe to play."

"They did not bring a book to read?" said Hendrick, putting up his sword.

"Oh, no. That we did not. In the winter, you read inside, in the solar, but if you were in the garden, you had to read the book inside and recite the tale outside."

Hendrick sat back. "I see I have gravely neglected my duties."

Both girls giggled. Marlene said, curiously, "Did the duke come to the garden?"

Sylvie's tongue touched her mouth. "All sorts of nobles did. I think the duke did. Once or twice, it was even when I was with my mother. I don't think he sang songs, though. Or told tales."

"Then I shall outdo him," said Hendrick grandly, leaning back and clasping his hands about one bent knee. "I shall tell a story."

"Like any peasant woman at her spinning," came a voice from the next cottage.

He did not even glance over. "Exactly so. Once upon a time, a king and queen had a son. Every year before Christmas, they set out fountains of wine and of oil in their courtyard, and anyone who wanted any could come and get some for the Christmas feast.

"One year, when the boy was seven, a witch came at the very end, just before the fountains were dry. She brought jugs and crawled into the fountains to get it all, down to the last drop, and as she came out, all smeared with oil and wine, the little prince laughed at her.

"She flew into a rage and declared he would never marry unless he found a maiden as beautiful as the day was long.

"The king and queen thought nothing of it, because they thought a witch so poor could not be so powerful, but the prince thought much of it. Finally, when his parents told him he had to marry, he said, 'I could not bear to marry, whether a princess or a noblewoman or a goose girl, if she were not so beautiful as the day is long. And if I have to seek for her for a year and a day, going past thrice ten kingdoms to find her, I will do so.'

"They remonstrated with him that he was their only heir, that such a bride had to be far away because they had never heard of her, that he might end up dead rather than married, but he would not be moved, and finally they gave him their blessing, and he set out with his sword and his horse, to search.

"No matter how far he rode, though he fought bears and wolves and giants, no one could tell him of a maiden as beautiful as the day was long, but one day, when traveling in the wilderness, he saw a bear chasing a fox, and the fox appealed to him, 'Help me, prince, and one day I may help you!' So he took after the bear with his sword and killed it, and the fox said, 'If ever you need my help, call for my friend the fox!'

"He rode on. The next day, he saw a salmon floundering beside a river, and he threw it back in, and the salmon said, 'If ever you need my help, call for my friend the salmon!'

"He rode on. The next day, he saw a raven caught in a tangle, and he freed it, and the raven said, 'If ever you need my help, call for my friend the raven!'

"He rode on, and the next day, he saw smoke rising from a chimney. He wondered if it were a woodcutter or a huntsman. He rode about the trees and the hills and found a rather large cottage on a hillside, with its garden about it. He went and knocked.

"'What are you doing here?' called a maiden from within, and her voice was like music. 'Do you not know that this is the home of a giant? He will return and eat you.'

"'I have faced giants before,' said the prince.

"'You can not face this one except to die,' said the maiden. 'He has no heart in his body.'

"'That will be as Heaven wills. As long as I have come this way, I will see what I may do.'

"The maiden opened the door, and she was as beautiful as the day was long, and the prince fell in love with her at once. She hid him in the storeroom and started to clean. Shortly thereafter, the giant returned, and sniffed the air, and said, 'I smell the blood of a man!'

"'I've been cleaning the room,' said the maiden. 'No wonder it smells, the way you splatter it all over the stones. It was stirred up by the cleaning.'

"So she cooked his dinner and as he nodded by the fire, she said, 'How lonely it is here! If you should die, I would die here, quite alone. You tell me that you do not have your heart in your body, but how do I know you keep it safe?'

"'It's buried under the threshold,' said the giant, but when he slept and woke and went off again, she and the prince dug and dug and dug under the threshold, and did not find it.

"So she put flowers and garlands over it, and told the giant that it was to honor it for keeping his heart safe, but she was afraid someone would dig it up. He laughed at her and told her it was under the hearth, and they dug and dug and dug and did not find the heart, and she put flowers and garlands over it, and the giant laughed again.

"'My heart is in an egg that is in a bird that is in a hare that is hidden in a box in a cottage that is seven hills away.'

"'Now I know that I am safe,' said the maiden, and in the morning the prince set out. He walked past seven hills, and found the cottage, and the box.

"He opened the box, and the hare fled, but the prince called, 'My friend the fox!' and the fox chased it down. No sooner than the fox had caught the hare than it opened its mouth and the bird flew out, but the prince called, 'My friend the raven!' and the raven chased it down. No sooner had the raven caught the bird than it dropped the egg into a lake, but the prince called, 'My friend the salmon!' and the salmon brought the egg up again.

"Then the fox and the raven and the salmon all told him to squeeze the heart in two, for the giant was not to be trusted. The prince did so, and the giant screamed from where he stood, and fell over dead, and the prince went back to the giant's house and brought back the maiden to his father's kingdom, where they married and lived happily ever after."

Marlene smiled, and some girls talked of what a wonderful prince he was. Hendrick smiled and said that he must see to the men keeping watch and left.

Within moments, Marlene looked at her sewing as if remembering something. "I have to—" She scrambled off, leaving her sewing as if she had forgotten it. Sylvie blinked, looking after her. Then, even in the royal garden, even in the very queen's presence, ladies had forgotten, sometimes, and had to run for things.

Sylvie sewed on. She wondered if Adelaide would find that she was making her stitches too fine. But then she finished, and frowned. Whatever did Marlene run off to do? She couldn't have gone to fetch something, not when it took this long.

Her frown deepening, she stood with cloth in hand. Lady Dagmar might object to this fuss as unbecoming curiosity—but how could she concentrate on keeping her stitches neat and even when she was distracted? She stood for a moment, her tongue touching her lips. She had other pieces here, to work on—but she could put away the mended piece to keep it safe.

She scuttled around the cottage, disturbing the flowers so that bees and butterflies flew off, and reached the door. In the shadows within, low voices spoke. Not Adelaide or Otto, she thought with a scowl, and stepped in.

Clothes lay spilled over the bed, from the chest: Adelaide's skirts, Otto's shirts. Marlene sat with Sylvie's gown of white and blue in her lap, solemnly talking with Hendrick about how they could not know Sylvie close enough that a girl her age in the gown could not fool them.

"And we do need the distraction," said Marlene.

Sylvie stared.

"And I look like the princess if you described her."

"That would be silly," said Sylvie, as crisply as she could, drawing both their gazes. "If they caught you dressed as me, they would not care that you were not me."

"It would buy some time," said Hendrick. "If they are all searching in one place."

Sylvie opened her mouth, closed it again, and opened it, feeling like a fish. "Time to do what? It's not like you could smuggle me away as long as they caught someone they thought was the princess."

"It might distract them long enough," said Hendrick.

"It might not," said Sylvie. "And that's why you didn't try it. The important thing is that the duke doesn't have me, or—" Her thoughts flew. "—someone he can claim is me to hold against the king. How could you smuggle the king a message that the girl the duke holds is not me? The king would do a great deal to protect the princess from the duke. And that is dangerous."

Marlene threw down the gown on the bed. "It's not as if we can wait for the winter and the spring thaw to make ways impassable to soldiers.

We can not last without the trade in herbs. There is so much that we buy that way. They grumble about it when they think children can not hear them speak."

Sylvie looked at both of them. Marlene looked defiant. Hendrick just looked unhappy.

"I shall have to speak with Master Gregor," said Sylvie. "At the manor court. To see what can be seen. He must hear much more than I do. Or you, either, Marlene."

"He doesn't know," said Hendrick. He sat back. "I perhaps should not tell you this, I perhaps should not know this, because he and my mother did not want me to hear this. But he does not know what to do. Your capture by the duke would doom us, but we can not remain trapped by the duke's forces. And there is still the question of how the soldiers turned out to find you, on that day."

A glittering possibility, snatched from her grasp. "We still could—" Sylvie eyed the dress.

They both watched her.

Sylvie shook her head. "No, the duke would know you within moments. He would question you about court and find out you know nothing of it. Like the bear who is promised a princess and figures out when he's given the peasant's daughter and the woodcutter's daughter quickly enough."

"I would know better than to answer what my father would do with a stand of trees."

Sylvie nodded. "But he would know better than to ask that. Would you know when the duke last arrived at court? What he petitioned for? Whom he snubbed?" She faltered a moment before plowing on. "He expected everyone to know everything about him. There was a rumor about his being angry with the chamberlain for not remembering something about his last visit."

Marlene looked mulish, and sulky. "We don't need to let them capture me."

"We can't stop them," said Sylvie. "If it weren't for the ghostweed luring them, they might have captured both of us. Heaven help us if we go and provoke them."

Hendrick looked taken aback.

"It will win us time, even if they did catch me," said Marlene.

Sylvie tried to remember anything that would help, and then she said, "You'd betray yourself before you opened your mouth." She grabbed the skirt. "These are court clothes. There's an art to wearing them so you don't look like a fool. They make fun of ladies who first come to court and are awkward. And you would have a harder time of it, because you'd be trying to walk through the woods."

Neither Marlene nor Hendrick looked convinced. Sylvie felt mulish and stupid. She was, after all, a princess. She had to think about the kingdom. Then—

"At the very least, we would need the Master of the Mountains to know. He's the one who would know where it would be best done if it were done at all."

Hendrick muttered something about woodmen.

"And to provide the guards to act at need," she said, triumphantly.

#

They woke early.

The moon was not yet full, but still had not yet set, and the stars blazed in all their numbers. And oh, how cold it was. Adelaide carefully dressed her and Marlene in heavy cloaks, but they shivered, huddling together. The guards were dark shadows except when they walked, briefly, in moonlight.

"This way," said the guard.

Sylvie knew the first part of the path, but soon they walked through hills and hollows she had never seen before. And would never recognize again, from this light. Even if, now and again, a dead tree loomed in the moonlight like an ogre.

The stars started to fade from the sky as they walked.

When a hall loomed ahead, Sylvie's breath came out in a gush. Everywhere, the sky was still black. The hall was more lit by torchlight than outlined by stars.

"Come in, come in," said a woman, more shadowed than lit. She stopped to embrace Hendrick, who murmured something. She stepped away, and the light fell on her. A tall woman, her hair golden where it was not touched with white.

Hendrick turned to Sylvie, hesitated, and spoke. "Your Highness, may I present my mother, Mistress Isabella."

Otto bowed, and Marlene and Adelaide curtsied, and Sylvie wavered and told herself that when she were here so people could see the princess, it would be silly to act like a peasant girl. Hendrick remembered to present his mother to her, and not her to his mother. She had to remember, too.

Mistress Isabella curtsied—rather well, if not up to court standards—and bustled them all within, saying they had made excellent time and were safely before any of the petitioners except those who had come last night. One guard talked of how the peasants in the village already talked about how the young master had visited the princess, and she had advised him how to deal with a giant.

"What is this?" said Mistress Isabella.

Marlene started to babble of the tale, and the details came out—more or less faithfully—as they were ushered to the back chambers.

Mistress Isabella sighed. "That he was there is true enough, and that rumor will suffice for trouble. This tale adds nothing. Except to make some wiser about rumor." But she did not look any happier, and at the sight of children peeping around the door at Sylvie, she sighed again but went to draw out a chair.

Sylvie sat. Snowfall hopped up in her lap.

"I suppose," said Adelaide sadly, "that there is nothing that can be told that they couldn't take as being about the princess."

"I could tell one," said Sylvie, brightly.

The servants' children edged closer. Marlene leaned forward. Adelaide glanced at Mistress Isabella.

"There will be some time before the court?"

Mistress Isabella closed her eyes and nodded.

"Once upon a time," said Sylvie, "a king and a queen had a son. One day, the king died, and the queen remarried. Her new husband was the son's regent. He heard that there was a forest in which no one ever hunted. He sent in huntsmen, and they never returned, until no more would go. He decreed that his son's inheritance should not be so marred. Whoever went into the forest and found why it was so dangerous would be richly rewarded.

"One day a man came with his dog and went hunting in the forest. His dog smelled something, and the man lay a net, and the net caught a wild man, all shaggy, and the man brought him back to the regent. From that day, anyone could go into the woods, but the regent ordered everyone out and said it was a royal hunting ground.

"And the regent threw the wild man into a cage and ordered that whoever opened that cage would die."

One child gave a shocked gasp.

"One day, when the regent went hunting, he ordered the prince excluded from the hunt on the grounds that he had been insolent. So the prince went to the cage and let the wild man out. The wild man snatched him up and fled. When the regent returned, he raged even when he heard it was the prince, but the prince was long gone."

Snowfall purred and rubbed against her hand. Sylvie petted her, and the children looked impatient.

"The wild man bore the prince off to the forest. There, in its heart, he brought him to an apple tree. It bore copper, silver, and golden apples, and the wild man told him to pick three. The prince picked three, one of each.

"'When I begged you to free me,' said the wild man, 'you freed me at once. You must listen to me again. Do not cut into these apples. Not for a day, not for a year. Not because you must drudge to earn your bread. When all is desperate, and only then, must you cut one.'"

Sylvie leaned forward. "'But once you cut one, the other two you may cut whenever you wish.'

"Then he carried him off to the next kingdom, put him down in sight of the castle, and told him to take whatever work they would give him. The prince went to the gate and humbly begged for work. They did not have so much as a job as a scullion, but he could work as the gardener's boy. So out into the garden he went, and he dug, and he hoed, and he weeded, and every morning he had to pick the flowers and present a bouquet to the princess, and every morning he bowed as he gave it.

"The princess saw he bowed more gracefully than many a courtier and wondered about him."

Some little boys scowled. Sylvie went on.

"Then the king was threatened by another king, and was greatly afraid because his army was small. But the soldiers gathered to defend the kingdom, and when the king led the army, and it marched off, the prince went to the apples and cut into the copper one.

"At once a troop of copper knights leapt up before him, and they brought him a suit of copper armor and a horse of copper. He armed himself and led the knights to the battle, where they fought valiantly—the prince the most valiantly of all—and routed the enemy. Then the prince rode away with the troop, dismissed the knights, and went back to being the gardener's boy.

"The king wished to reward his kingdom's deliverer, and held a tournament, in hopes that the strange knight would show his prowess there, as well. He declared it was to find his daughter's bridegroom, since the champion of the war had fled.

"On the day of the tourney, the prince brought the princess her bouquet of flowers, and she said to him that she would prefer the rose given by the greatest knight in the tourney to the lady he deemed most beautiful."

Snowfall meowed. Sylvie scratched her behind the ears.

"The prince bowed and said that would be as it would be, but when he left her, he took out the silver apple and cut into it. At once squires leapt up before him and brought him a suit of silver and a horse of silver. He went to the tourney and fought valiantly, and at the end, he gave the princess the rose and rode off too swiftly for the king's knights to catch him.

"So the king held another tourney, and the prince used the golden apple, and the king's knights fought more fiercely, so that the prince's foot was wounded, but he still won, still gave the princess the rose, and still rode off.

"The princess told her father she could lead him to the knight. Then she led him out into the garden and to the hut where the gardener's boy slept, and showed them how he had bound the wound on his foot.

"So the prince and the princess married, and when his stepfather heard that the prince had a magical band of knights, he fled the kingdom, and so they reigned over that one as king and queen, and when her father died, they reigned over his, too."

One little boy said, "The duke brought soldiers."

"But," said Mistress Isabella, reproving, "he did not bring them to aid his king. Only to fight him."

"Like the other king in the story," said Sylvie.

The boy scowled.

"Besides," said Sylvie, "he brought them too soon. He hasn't helped a wild man or run away to another kingdom, let alone taken a position as a gardener's boy."

His eyes widened, and his mouth popped open. The other children started to babble about it, and one girl looked aside.

"Would you take a job as a gardener's boy?"

Sylvie glanced over. Hendrick stood there.

"I would have more fortune as a herb-gatherer," said Hendrick. "But, come now, would I have to run away from my father? Or even my stepfather, were such a thing to come to pass? My mother has better judgment than that queen."

The girl nodded in content. Hendrick looked at Sylvie.

"Your Highness, my father wishes to seat you in the hall even now. The first petitioners are arriving, and the longer you are there, the longer they will have to see you."

"To gawk," said Mistress Isabella.

Sylvie stood. Without enthusiasm, she said, "Being gawked at is a princess's first duty."

"First we will give them something to gawk at," said Mistress Isabella. "Adelaide, Otto, if you go into the hall, she will be ready shortly."

She ushered Sylvie into a room. Off in the corner, little boys practiced their bows, and little girls their curtsies, before Mistress Isabella sent them running about on errands.

#

This new, green gown was neither so fancy nor so well-fitting as any gown she had worn at court. Mistress Isabella's maids fussed over trying to take it in a bit, but within minutes, Mistress Isabella swept up.

"It is well enough," she declared. "Everyone knows she fled the duke's men without her wardrobe."

Sylvie glanced down. "I do not look like a peasant girl," she said, "and that's the important thing."

Mistress Isabella smiled before hurrying off with more to prepare. The maids brought Sylvie down toward the hall, and at the door, they curtsied and left.

Sylvie felt uneasy but slipped into the hall. Smaller than the royal hall, and less adorned, it was quite large enough next to the cottages. From the doorway, Sylvie looked about as surreptitiously as she could. Scattered villages could yield many men and women, and already they clumped here and there.

And she could not stand about like this, hiding in the shadows. Her purpose was to show herself. Otto was already looking about for her, and Adelaide had put her foot down on propriety.

Walk, she told herself. Like a princess.

She drew many glances and thought it would be easier in the sweeping gown, with a coronet, to remind her that princesses her age did not scamper, but she walked up to them at a sedate pace.

Adelaide smiled at her. Marlene looked anxious. Mistress Isabella swept up behind her and urged all three of them to sit with her and sew while Otto stood with the men.

Otto bowed and left. Mistress Isabella crossed the room to the two chairs and the stools. One chair stood higher than the other, on a dais. Adelaide and Marlene went for the stools as Sylvie braced herself, climbed up the step, and sat in the higher chair. Snowfall bounded up and snuggled beside her.

Mistress Isabella sat with the calm of a shepherdess on the grass, taking up her sewing to wile away the hours until sheep needed to be rescued from folly, or led back to the fold. Sylvie took her own sewing and supposed there were worse descriptions. People moved about the room like sheep about a meadow, eyeing her, and if not bleating, murmuring to each other about the sight.

Marlene shifted.

"It's all part of being a princess," said Sylvie, her voice low. She took another stitch. "Being seen."

"I suppose," said Marlene. She looked at her sewing. "All the more after you've been in danger."

Sylvie's needle hesitated. One man nearby had a bandage on his head, and noticing him, she saw others. Men limping. Men with arms in slings.

She looked back at her sewing and took a stitch. She did not know they had suffered their injuries while looking for her. She took another. Then, they might have been injured by the soldiers elsewhere. She swallowed.

The crowds shifted. That was familiar from the royal court, and Sylvie looked up. People moved into position before the high seat, and Gregor emerged. Hendrick solemnly stood at his right hand, and the petitioners filed forward.

Sylvie listened.

She had listened to her own father hold manor court, for his demesne lands, and she could see the commonalities. Sometimes even the same things. Stray cows. A bridge and whose duty was it to keep it up, anyway. Others—she meditatively took a stitch. Her father heard cases about firewood, but not about herbs growing wild. Certainly not ones in which a woman claimed that she had just happened on what a man said was his garden, and the lond had been so nice, she had to dig it, or accusations were thrown of digging redroot out of season.

That one grew so heated that Mistress Isabella paused to explain that redroot grew its seeds in the fall, and so had to be harvested after that, or it would fail.

"Not that it doesn't fail sometimes even when they do wait," said Adelaide.

Mistress Isabella rolled her eyes. "So true."

A man strode into the room, his footfalls echoing. The crowd shifted, to let him through. Dust and mud stained, as if he had traveled far and in haste.

"A messenger?" murmured Mistress Isabella, taking a stitch. "He might have word of the duke's men moving."

Neither Marlene's needle nor Adelaide's moved.

The man reached a clear view of the high seat and bowed deeply. Then he swiveled toward Mistress Isabella and bowed still more deeply.

Not Mistress Isabella. Her. Sylvie gulped.

"Your Royal Highness. Master of the Mountains. News has come from downriver. His Royal Majesty has roused his forces and descended on the duchy in force. Even with the soldiers he sent here, the duke would have been hard put to withstand him."

"How wonderful!" exclaimed a woman, and the hall resounded with the babble of what it might mean. No one heeded Master Gregor except that as Master Gregor beckoned, the messenger came up beside him.

Snowfall purred. Sylvie could only feel it, not hear it, in this uproar. She wondered what the man said to Master Gregor. Neither man looked happy.

Her gaze moved about. Some peasants already looked cantankerous at the delay. Those closest to her muttered complaints that their cases still had to be heard, whatever mischief happened in the lowlands.

Sylvie looked back at her sewing. Snowfall wriggled, and she went to pet her. She wondered if she could sew neatly enough. It was not just a matter of waiting out the tiresome hours with patience. Her finger went over the seam. All wars were times of danger. She might find that the next message was that she was queen. Or perhaps that the duke had captured her father, instead of her.

She stared out at the hall, but she did not see it, or the peasants in it.

Mistress Isabella picked up the vest she sewed. "Life will go on. We will need any news as swiftly as it can be obtained."

How calm she sounded. Like a queen.

Sylvie nodded and tried to match her. Like a princess. "I wonder what the duke will do."

"Won't the king catch him?" said Marlene.

"He'll try," said Sylvie. "But—the duke tried to catch me."

Master Gregor's voice rose sharply over the clamor. "Captain Edmund. Go and warn the guards that they may have to move without warning, and I will be grateful for their readiness to do so swiftly."

A great golden bear of a man bowed to the Master of the Mountains, and left.

"All my people must keep watch for any danger," said Master Gregor. "Nevertheless, our work must go on through such watch. I will hear the next case."

A man walked forward with a case of a dispute about trespass by a cow. He did not seem thankful for the judgment against him, but the air in the hall began to ease.

Slowly, the court proceeded through the other cases. With far more sidelong glances at Sylvie. Every now and again, someone said something about the lovely young princess.

She managed to take a few more stitches that were not actually dreadful. She wondered if she should have learned more about laws, and whether she could have. She had heard her father's manor courts, and she did not think she knew these laws.

"The law does not apply so loosely," said a woman, sounding desperate. "The law of the mountain does not apply in the pass there. The law of Greenbridge applies, and I may gather the berries by it."

She whirled around. "Is that not so, Your Highness?"

Everyone looked at her. She could not bring down her hand, caught with needle in the air. Her heartbeat drummed in her ears, and no one looked away.

Sylvie managed to find her tongue. "Even under Greenbridge law, there would still be questions about whether you might gather. You can not merely invoke it and claim all is allowed."

"At that," said Master Gregor, "under Greenbridge law, the first question is whether you invoked mountain law on it."

That apparently was quickly settled. Sylvie was not even asked to confirm that the woman had forfeited any claim to Greenbridge law by having invoked mountain law in the past. Then, thought Sylvie, sewing again, everyone knew that.

As the cases drew to a close, Mistress Isabella said, her voice low, "Master Gregor will want to speak with you, Your Highness. After."

Sylvie nodded. Adelaide looked anxious, and Marlene puzzled, but they waited. Then Mistress Isabella drew her out of the great hall, past the great chamber, into the empty second chamber.

She brought in food for them to eat, cold meat and sweet tarts and cider. "It has been longer than we expected. I think many cases would not have been heard yet, or been settled before they came to court."

"Except they wanted to see the princess," said Otto, heavily.

Sylvie ate eagerly. It had been longer than she had thought it would be. It was hard on Otto and Adelaide, and Marlene, eating beside her.

She swallowed the last of a peach tart. "At least, that means fewer cases for the next court."

A groan sounded from the doorway. "May Heaven so grant," said Master Gregor. "But I doubt it." He came in, with Hendrick in tow, and both of them took food and ate, but Master Gregor spoke over it.

"This is not over."

"Merow!" called Snowfall.

"And we are indeed grateful to you, Mistress—Snowfall. But— " He shook his head. "If I had not ventured to the riverside in search of news, I would have been here when news came of the soldiers, searching. Instead of its falling to Hendrick. Again."

Hendrick's gaze was modestly downcast. Mistress Isabella murmured that it was, after all, the young master's duty, though he had risen to it admirably.

Sylvie felt cold and sluggish, but she reminded herself that it was indeed dangerous.

"There is something that might be the third time," said Sylvie. And told how she had found Hendrick and Marlene plotting.

Marlene turned scarlet as she spoke, and Otto looked grim and composed, and Adelaide as if she would smack Marlene for her folly were she not before the Master of the Mountains.

Hendrick stared at the floor.

Master Gregor stood like stone. Her own father would have envied him his composure. Silence fell, and moments passed.

Finally, Master Gregor sighed. "Let us hope that it does not come to that."

Sylvie felt horrified. Too chilled to move. Hadn't the Master of the Mountains listened to her?

"Heaven blessing your father with victory, it may not matter. But it may. The soldiers may grow desperate with the duke's defeat. And it is unwise to rule out in advance what may be needed to defend against them." He glanced at her. "You are right, Your Highness, in that that proposal would be a matter of desperation."

In the silence after, he ate a little more. Then he looked up.

"Many villagers have already left, but, Your Highness, please walk among those left as you go to leave yourself. Let them all see you."

"Again," said Otto, sourly, taking up a piece of cheese. "Perhaps it will stick."

#

"We must go swiftly," said Adelaide, and led the way to the front door, through the crowds. Many people bowed or curtsied before staring at her like a golden lion brought from a far off land.

Some wondered whether she worked as a scullery maid here. Mutely, she looked at her hands. A scullery maid would have hands all red and chapped from washing. She had marks where she had pricked herself with her needle. No, she was not a scullery maid. She was a seamstress, earning her living with her needle.

Except that she probably was not. She could help, but she doubted that her sewing covered her keep.

She trailed dutifully after Adelaide, out into sunlight already tinged with orange by evening, and onto the way. They passed the fields and reached the forest, and the light dimmed, not so much from passing time as the thick leaves.

"At least my father," said Sylvie, "won't believe the tale about my going up a chimney."

Marlene shifted. "He might believe you were a scullery maid."

"Then," said Adelaide, "he would go to the Master of the Mountains, who could set him straight." She pulled in her skirt as they went about brush encroaching on the path. "After all, who else in the mountains has so many servants as to hire a scullery maid?"

When they emerged into the valley, the sky was flowering in red and orange, and the shadows were deep.

#

The next night, by the fire, Sylvie leaned against the hearthstones and said, "We should pack. Not much. A few things. To help us escape."

"And carry them with us at all times?" said Otto. "That would be awkward."

The fire sighed as the last of a log burned through and sank down on the coals.

"It would be worse if we ran back to get them," said Adelaide, gently. "You did not go back to the castle at all. As soon as you saw the soldiers, you ran." She spread her hands. "Still it might be wise to prepare some things. Food perhaps. It could be concealed."

"We could hide them in the forest?" said Marlene.

"It might be easier to circle about to get them," said Otto, "but if they are hidden well enough that no one steals them, they will be hard to find."

He reached for the shovel to bank the fire. "Sleep, though, will aid us without such danger."

#

Sylvie sewed.

Bees bumbled from flower to flower in the garden, with the hives all humming behind the cottages. Cats, with Snowfall in their number, stalked about the houses. Villagers—those not out of sight, busy in field or pasture or forest—bustled with tasks from drying mushrooms to churning butter. And sewing lay beside her, ready for mending.

Sylvie tied off a thread.

"Do they really embroider handkerchiefs for messages?" said Marlene, after a minute. "At court?"

"They try," said Sylvie. "They have all sorts of books of messages, except the books don't always agree." A little girl ran by, and Sylvie smiled. "I was a little younger than her when I tried to make my parents handkerchiefs with messages. And I did not embroider them with roses, where most people agree. My father graciously accepted the handkerchief and told Lady Dagmar to show me the books."

She cut off another thread.

"What was the message you sent?"

"Childish," said Sylvie. "I told them I loved them. My mother graciously accepted and told me that I did not have to keep it secret." She sighed and took another stitch. "It was none too neatly done, either."

She could tell them again, soon, she told herself, with speech and not stitches. And she could not sacrifice cloth to such silliness.

A shout made her stitch go awry. Marlene was already staring at the clump of people gathering around—where a path ended. They moved wildly, slowly shifting toward the village as new people gathered.

Sylvie swallowed. So wildly that she could not tell who arrived. They gathered, abandoning their work as if it meant no more to them than a lady courtier's fancy work. The gabbling was so frantic that she could not make out anything they said, only how distressed they were.

She wondered if she could wiggle through the crowd and get close enough to hear what the news was.

"What is the princess doing here?" A woman stood from the crowd and pointed.

The silence that followed was so complete that Sylvie heard the bees buzzing, and that Snowfall was not purring.

"It's not safe, it's not safe." The woman looked about. "What if the king hears that we kept her here without troubling our heads about it? He'll know we knew."

"What is the news?" said Otto, his voice commanding, as he came up behind Sylvie and Marlene.

"The duke," said a travel-stained woman, and stopped from breath.

"Yes, Pierrette?"

"He did not wait for the king and his forces, let alone battle. He fled up the river with all of his forces. He is searching for the princess."

"And," said the woman who had pointed out Sylvie, "it's not like it will be dangerous for him. No snow or sleet or hail to trouble his travels. No flood or fire. He can hunt the hills through. Having her here is such a danger."

"To the princess?" said a man with a sneer. "Or to you?"

To all of us, thought Sylvie, feeling icy cold.

"Doesn't do any good to drive her off," said an old man, hobbling out. "Worse, even." At the outcry, he snorted. "The duke's men would ransack the village for her. If she's not here, it's the worse for us. Plans must be made better than that."

"I'm sure we'll be as chubby as acorn-fed pigs," said another man, "after the duke's men come through."

"They've done no great harm yet," said a thin woman.

"They were afraid of causing too much trouble," said the old man. "With the duke breathing down their backs, they will be far bolder—afraid of *him*. I doubt that any man of them will try to flee the duke and the mountains."

Sylvie said, sharply, "Has anyone sent word to the Master of the Mountains?"

Everyone looked at her as if a cat had spoken. She glared back. Someone had to think. Didn't any of them realize that if Master Gregor dealt with the matter, it would be done?

"She is the princess," said Otto from behind her. His voice was very deep, even deeper than when the messenger had arrived. "Do you know better than she does?"

With much grumbling, people turned away. Then Sylvie noticed.

"Who is going?"

People stopped as if turned to stone. No one said a word. And no one looked as if to leave. Her tongue touched her lip. She had spoken more harshly than she had meant to. But she had to say it. And say this as well.

"It would be cruel," said Sylvie, "to send on the messenger who brought us the news. And unwise, because haste is needed. But that means that someone else must go."

Now, her voice sounded thin in her own ears.

Someone grumbled that they had just been to manor court and hadn't the Master of the Mountains got anyone else to tell him, and one boy, younger than Hendrick, said, "I'll go!"

"Excellent, Florian," said Otto.

#

"He just did that to make a lass fancy him," grumbled Ellen. "He should have been back by now. That's not going to make her fancy him. No lass's silly enough to fancy a lad who runs away from his work. At least not a lass who'd I let marry him."

Sylvie looked at the shadows. Where Snowfall and Dawn now slumbered. She would not say so, for fear of encouraging Ellen, but Florian could, in fact, have gotten to the hall and back by now. She thought.

"He did have to deliver the message," she said. "The Master of the Mountains might have questions."

"Then—" Ellen pointed at her. "You should have sent Pierrette! She came with the news. She could have told him more."

Sylvie took another stitch. Then a shout broke into the village, starting women and girls from their sewing and spinning. Old men looked up from whittling, and younger ones from chopping wood and fixing fences.

More shouts rose, louder than when Pierrette arrived. Sylvie stood. Her heart pattered. She had to find out whether she was in danger and should flee, she told herself, that was more needful than the sewing she did—

In the thick of the crowd, and the clamor, it took her a moment to recognize them. The Master and Mistress of the Mountains, and the young master, had dressed for a journey in the mountains, and to avoid gazes.

But the exclamations betrayed them before she saw their faces.

"What happened?" she called.

Someone noticed her, and Master Gregor walked forward, still catching his breath. They must have traveled quite hard.

His voice was clipped as he spoke. "We had barely got your message when the duke arrived with his men. They had heard a tale that the princess worked as a scullery maid in our kitchen."

"We lost them," said Mistress Isabella. "They were not suited for some of the less even lands." She smiled a little.

"They were swearing the rocks were jagged," said one woodsman, and laughter resounded.

Sylvie swallowed.

"That will not last long," said Hendrick. "The soldiers faced worse the night they almost caught the princess, and the duke is desperate enough to listen. We had to leave the messenger to rest in a village, because he could not keep up with us." He looked at his sleeves. One was torn as if by a branch. "It was just as well that we headed for the forest that morning. And—we have to do something to prevent his success."

"The king is coming," said Mistress Isabella.

"The duke knows that. That is why the danger is so great." Hendrick looked grim. "We are not his match. Not if he brings his forces to bear."

"The king is," said Dennis, scornfully.

"The king," said Master Gregor, "does not know the mountains. He does not even have soldiers who spent their time hunting about it for the princess. And—he does not know that the duke has a spy in his court. A maid heard them talk, of this spy, this man. They call him Beorn."

"We must send word to the king," said Hendrick. He looked about. For her, Sylvie guessed.

"Only if we can get past the spy," said Master Gregor, gently.

"This is hopeless," said Bess. "We can not defeat the duke's men. By the time the king's men arrive, they will be so scattered over the hills that they can escape. And we can not escape them!"

Sylvie's heartbeat started to drum in her ears. Loud enough to drown out the talk about her. Until someone spoke of smuggling the princess to the king.

"No," she said, firmly, loudly, startling them all into silence. She gulped. She had read the history books about battles. "What we need is for the duke's forces to be drawn together. Somewhere unwise for them to be."

She looked about. "When I was gathering herbs, you used the cliff to get me away from his soldiers when they were within earshot. Can you find someplace where another force could attack them with more ease than they can be attacked?"

Silence fell. Her heart hammered again. Dumbstruck faces looked at her. For all the books told of how important battle sites were, she did not know how to pick one.

"Your Highness," said Master Gregor heavily, "there is no place from which my men could defeat them. Even if we could bring them together."

"Are there places where the king's men could?"

Then she looked about.

"If the duke's men come here, they will know something happened. Let the Master, the Mistress, and the young master come inside, with me." She waved a hand. "Go about your business. You are safest so."

Ellen grumbled.

Sylvie turned toward her. "Go."

Master Gregor spoke in a low voice to a man as the villagers pulled back, and they worked their way over.

Once they were inside, the cottage was awkwardly close. Sylvie sat on the bed. Snowfall climbed into her lap and purred. Sylvie tried to pet her, awkwardly, while watching the door. Adelaide did not stir up the dull red of the fire, and the only light came through the windows and door.

Marlene came over and sat on the floor, her back against the bed. No one spoke.

Master Gregor loomed in the doorway, his shadow cutting off the light. Then he pulled the door shut, dimming the light to just what the windows gave.

He said, heavily, "I set men to keep an eye for eavesdroppers. Perhaps, Your Highness, it will be obvious to anyone who passes by, but—" He spread his hands. "We have to risk it."

Adelaide shifted.

"And the rest of the village is about their work. It may not fool a stranger. But I doubt that ordering them about would make it more convincing."

Adelaide moved over, to stand with her back to the wall, next to the bed.

Sylvie nodded, as gravely as she could. "There are two things that we can do. The first is to send a messenger to my father."

"The spy will hear of that," said Master Gregor.

"Not if he—my father—sets guards against eavesdroppers," said Sylvie.

"And why," said Mistress Isabella, "would he set such guards?"

Sylvie let her breath out. "I will need a fine white handkerchief, and to embroider it in black and red. That will serve as a token."

Marlene squeaked. "The messages!"

"I think," said Sylvie, "that I will just match the one I gave him before. So he can recognize it."

She glanced among them. "Perhaps it would be best if the young master bore the message."

"Perhaps," said Mistress Isabella, more coldly. "But what good is the messenger if not to bear a message?"

Sylvie drew in a deep breath. Her father the king, and the Master of the Mountains, and the young master, had all faced the duke's forces. She could face these people here.

"Tell him where he should array his forces to attack the duke's men in force. Master Gregor must choose this place. Somewhere that the king's men can reach more quickly than the duke can gather his. My token will tell my father to listen to him."

"And why," said Master Gregor, "would the duke gather his men? Let alone in a place of my choosing. They can not search so well altogether."

Sylvie drew in a deep breath again. "Because," she said, and her voice sounded weak to her, "he thinks he can catch the princess."

"He's thought that all along," said Otto.

"This time, we must give him reason to think that he can succeed. And soon. Let him see the princess. Arrayed in white and blue and visible in the forest."

Adelaide gasped, and pulled Sylvie to her. "It's too dangerous. Let's have none of this talk of your gadding about like that."

"But—but I *am* in danger," said Sylvie. She raised her head. "Everyone is in danger. The duke has burned his bridges and has no other hope. There is nothing he will not do for his own safety. He'd burn down every village in the mountains, with the villagers inside."

Marlene said, "He won't see *you*, he'll see your dress. You don't have to do it yourself." She raised her head. "And it's not like it would win time to do nothing."

"It's not just my safety," said Sylvie. "It's the whole kingdom's. If—if he gets close enough, I might have to speak to him, to taunt him into coming nearer, into the trap."

Mistress Isabella muttered it would be wise to spread rumors that they would bring the princess to the king, to start their gathering.

"And once they've started to gather," said Master Gregor. He shook his head. "If you're close enough to speak, you're close enough for an archer to hit."

Sylvie spread her hands. "Heaven grant that we escape that. But they could come close enough to catch me without the king's army being near."

Snowfall sat up, and rubbed against her arm.

"Only if you bring the kitten with you," said Adelaide, faintly. "I won't allow it otherwise."

Snowfall purred.

Chapter 8: The Cloth

Every stitch has to be perfect, Sylvie told herself. Every stitch.

She held the cloth out into the sunshine, and reminded herself that she had not memorized the original handkerchief. She had to hope to get it close enough. Master Gregor and Mistress Isabella were sending the message and stirring up the rumors. She had to do her part.

Marlene argued with her mother again, that Snowfall had followed them out into the forest when she was needed, but Adelaide was adamant—and the handkerchief had to be done, whatever anyone did or argued about.

Sylvie bit her lip. The messages along the edge were done, but the flower—she had forgotten how long it took to stitch it. She had gotten the outline done.

A man came running across the village, heading into the cottage. For a moment, she wavered. Master Gregor could deal with his own men. She could not even guess where they should lure the duke's men.

Then, she had proposed this whole matter.

She stuck the needle into the cloth and stood, to walk over to the cottage. The men's voices rose in heated argument, but when she opened the door, the mere light silenced them. They all looked over. Some scowled at the sight of her.

"What has happened?"

"The king is moving too far away," said the messenger, biting out the words. "Within a day or two, it will be all but impossible to get him to a good place without the duke realizing what we are doing."

Her heart started to beat harder in her chest. "Then," she said, slowly, "we will have to get a message to him sooner."

The messenger rolled his eyes.

She turned to Master Gregor, and Hendrick, and held out the handkerchief. "I have outlined everything." Her voice sounded thin in her own ears, and she tried to make it stronger. "The messenger will have to persuade the king that it is truly mine even though it does not match perfectly—" Her gaze moved among them. "He should be able to recognize the flower."

Master Gregor took it from her fingers. "And you have left the needle in it."

Sylvie nodded.

Master Gregor gave it to Hendrick. "Take it and go. We will go with the princess, within an hour."

Hendrick nodded and left the cottage. Sylvie blinked, and Master Gregor turned to her.

"We won't have time for you to dress as the princess once we are there. You will put the dress on here, and we will cover it up."

Sylvie opened her mouth. Then she shut it again. It would be Master Gregor and his men who had to keep her unseen until the right time, and then seen again.

#

Did she have to wear so heavy a cloak? It weighed on her shoulders, and worse, it was so hot with all the walking she had done since she had left the village.

She sighed. An hour to leave. Then hours upon hours upon *hours* of walking. And it was hot.

Even here, in shade where sunlight never pierced the leaves for as much as a fleck of light on the dead leaves. She shifted her weight, but nothing made it cooler.

She tried to watch for the men, but between the shadows and how they moved, she could not see them. She could not hear them, either. She heard more from Adelaide, waiting beside her without speaking. And from the faint breezes, and the occasional squirrel running through the dead leaves.

Adelaide let her breath out. Perhaps she resented how long this took, and whether they should have come this early, with nothing to do but wait. And wait. And wait.

She envied Snowfall, who napped in the basket in perfect contentment. She tried to tell herself that it was a good sign and tried to not clutch the basket handle too tightly.

Adelaide started beside her. "Take off your cloak," she said, sharply.

Sylvie obeyed in surprise, and Adelaide snatched it up, folding it with haste. She felt abruptly chilly in the shade.

A man loomed up before them. Three men. One nodded to Adelaide and said, his voice low, that it was time to leave. The biggest of them scooped Sylvie up as easily as if she were a babe in arms. She squeaked and pulled the basket to herself, and the man, ignoring her motion, strode off. Adelaide scrambled after.

The man all but ran. He would run himself ragged at this rate, let alone Adelaide. His heart hammered, and so did hers, caught in the fright.

Snowfall peeked upward, and then curled up, back in the basket.

For a moment, she thought she saw a man, a soldier in red, but only an unclear glimpse in the thickets, and not only because she was all but lying in the man's arms.

The man scrambled down a hill and up another, branches and leaves brushing by. Her heart hammered and barely slowed again when he stopped and turned her about, to put her down.

She stood at a clifftop. The breeze tugged at her white skirt. Snowfall slept in the basket.

"They saw her," said the man, "they definitely saw her. They came together faster than I dreamed they could."

"They heard the rumors," said another, grimly, speaking to the other men and not to her. Adelaide reached them, huffing for breath.

The men started to talk about how at least the king's men moved into place, they could hope they had gotten the message.

Sylvie's gaze went over the slopes. The trees were thick, but she thought it was a gentle slope on one side, and cliffs on the other.

"And what are you thinking, Sylvie?" said Adelaide.

"That any soldiers who are caught against the cliff are in trouble."

Silence followed. She tried to remember if any of the men had been talking.

"If it comes to that, they will," said the man who carried her. "But there's a gorge ahead. We hope to carry you up it, and trap them there."

Another man, lean and wiry, snorted. "It's not big enough. We'll end up fighting many of them out here."

"If we get the duke," said the first man, "the rest will scatter. Already there are so many tales of men who flee."

"I thought the whole point of this was gather them together," said the lean man.

Snowfall's head peeked over the basket. Then, with a merow, she leapt out and onto the forest floor, darting through bracken. Sylvie was so startled she dropped the basket, and Adelaide began to call to Snowfall. Snowfall turned into a glimpse of white among the ferns.

A man appeared, down in the valley, and made a sharp gesture with his hand. The man snatched her up again and ran. He held her far more tightly, and the run down the slope was far more jolting. Branches slapped at her.

Worse, shouts came from behind her.

She cringed and bit her lip, and fought to keep from whimpering. Even when her foot brushed against rock. Even as the rock pressed in to either side, and the man shifted to holding her head toward the gorge.

"I can walk," she said.

After a hesitant moment, he put her down. She scrambled, there being only one way to climb. Her hands were covered with dirt within moments, and she scraped her hand within a moments. She ignored the blood and climbed. The shouts grew louder behind her. An ugly scream, like a man mortally wounded by arrow.

Faster, she told herself. You, and the men, are safer the more quickly you reach the top. She stared at the stone, and could not see her next handhold for a moment. Then she grabbed a fern and climbed a step.

A man reached over from beside her and pulled her out, to stand her on the stone and reach to help the next man. Archers already shot at the duke's men. Another man put an arm on her hand and tugged her away, as the man who had carried her climbed up.

Loud shouts, "What folly is this, letting her get away?"

Sylvie slowly turned her head to face the voice. He dressed like the duke, he shouted imperiously like the duke, he even bore his coat of arms, but—

"That's not the duke!"

Her shrill words echoed louder than she would have dreamed they could. Gazes turned toward her about the forest, both the woodsmen and the duke's soldiers.

"You infamous liar!" His sword pointed at the cliff. "There's the wicked princess. Capture her! Do not let her get away!"

His men eyed the stones, as if reckoning how expensive the attack would be, and eased back.

"If you are the duke, tell me what befell when you went into the rose garden when last you visited court!"

"You insolent brat! Talking so wildly! You should know to hold your tongue about what your elders do! You shouldn't have been in the garden when your elders were there!"

Sylvie drew a deep breath and shouted as loud as she could. "The duke didn't go into the garden! He saw that I was there and said it should be left to little children!"

A man pulled her back from the cliff, out of sight.

One huntsman whispered, "Is it true?"

"Of course it's true," shouted Sylvie. "You can tell that he has none of the men who came to court with him, because they would know it was true."

Arrows flew behind her, and the man walked on. Ahead were men in uniforms.

"Those are the king's men," she called. "Turn me about so I can prove I'm the princess."

A shout of laughter came from the woods. "That's the clever lass who scared off half the duke's men?"

"Send for a courtier," said a man in a deeper voice. "You, Robin. And run. There can be clever treachery. And lasses who wear the princess's dress."

"With treachery or without," said another man.

"There are enough of the duke's men to fight still," said Master Gregor, coming up. "Imprudent to mingle our forces, but less so to not fight them."

"They're fleeing now."

"Wise of them," said a grave voice that caused Sylvie's head to jerk about. He wouldn't come this close, would he? "Outwitted by a princess who will, in time, grace the throne as a wise and prudent queen, but for now is still a child."

"Papa!" shouted Sylvie, and ran across the forest floor. Guards moved about them, but she did not stop before she threw her arms about her father's neck. He held her tight for a moment, and then freed her to look about.

Master Gregor was embracing Hendrick, and Sylvie giggled.

"Now we must catch the duke!" she said.

#

She was not allowed near the search.

Her father and Master Gregor conferred briefly and gravely and turned to Hendrick.

"I must remain with the king," said Master Gregor. "Much must be done. Therefore, it is only fitting that the young master escort the princess to the Master's hall. I will send fitting forces with you."

"What about Adelaide?" said Sylvie.

In the moment's pause, a loud meow was heard. Sylvie looked over to see Snowfall leaping from Adelaide's arms to bound toward her. With a squeak, Sylvie dropped down to catch her and stood with the kitten in her arms. Snowfall purred.

"So this is the fabled Queen Angelique's kitten," said her father, dryly.

Adelaide curtsied.

"And Snowfall led Adelaide to safety!" said Sylvie triumphantly.

Adelaide, straightening, smiled.

Her father smiled back and told Master Gregor to send men with them, Adelaide as well as herself, under Hendrick's charge.

"Should I wear my mantle again? To cover up?" said Sylvie. Her nose wrinkled. "It's hot."

"That will not be necessary," said Master Gregor. "With the men coming and going, the path to the hall is as clear as any path can be. And if the duke's men do appear, you will need to run more easily."

"Merow!" said Snowfall.

#

Ferns and bushes hedged the path tightly around. They had always to walk single file, and sometimes, with Snowfall purring in her arm, Sylvie wished she had two hands free to pull her skirt loose. Once Adelaide had to help her. When the height of one hill revealed the hall, standing ahead, Sylvie felt very glad.

The hall bustled with more people than when Master Gregor had held court. More men, and most of them in the prime of life, and heavily armed. All of them about their work as if—the duke had brought his men-at-arm into the mountains, and they might be needed to defend the hall.

They should have guards on watch, thought Sylvie, and they started to descend.

Someone shouted, and pointed. More shouts followed, of surprise and glee, and men moved about, some heading up the path, and Sylvie made out something about white.

"I don't think they spotted you," said Sylvie to Snowfall. Snowfall purred.

Hendrick hailed them at a careful distance, and men came up to join their escort in. When she could be seen from the hall itself, cheers for the princess's safety rose, loud enough to alert to any of the duke's men.

Sylvie giggled. Too late. The duke did not have enough men to seize her.

Some perplexed cries had the largest of the men-at-arms lifting her, and Snowfall, to his shoulder, where she gleamed in the sunlight. Shouts resounded from the mountains. Enough to frighten off even an army.

From her height, she saw Mistress Isabella rushing from the hall. She tried to call to her, and though her words were drowned out, the woman realized where Hendrick would be. She pushed through the crowd as the man at arms lowered Sylvie.

She burst out to greet them, exclaiming over their safety, fussing almost as much over Sylvie as over Hendrick.

"Come inside," she said. She urged them toward the door, saying they should eat and rest, but before they reached it, another man came running down the hill.

He stopped several strides up the slope, and panted for breath. Then he shouted, "The duke!" He dragged in a deep breath. "The duke has been captured!"

In the uproar, Sylvie stepped closer to Mistress Isabella. She thought, from the clamor, that he had been caught while cowering in a hollow tree.

"Lucky for him that he was caught," murmured Adelaide. "He does not know the forest."

"He was running away," said one little boy, shrilly. "He wanted to get a job as a gardener's boy in a foreign country, but he didn't have the three magic apples!"

Laughter resounded, all around. A girl started to talk about whether there was a wild man to free, and be carried off by. Adelaide rolled her eyes.

Chapter 9: The King

Mistress Isabella, sitting in the sunlight several days later, sewed with perfect calm despite the voices coming out the open door. Adelaide occasionally muttered at the cloth. Sylvie kept on mending and hoped no one noticed that she sewed more slowly than usual, though, she told herself, her stitches were still neat.

Marlene tried to thread her needle again. "How do you manage to sew when they are in council like that?"

Sylvie thought for a moment, remembering. "Usually they're in another room. Far away." She took another stitch. She might learn about such talk days later. She thought they had talked about her going to the mountains three days before anyone told her. But here, when they were so loud, and the matter was so close to her. . . .

She stabbed her needle into her work. Just as she had done with the handkerchief, she remembered as she stood up. "I need a basket."

#

Lord Leonard stood with his back to the door as he declaimed. The men before him noticed her arrival, basket under her arm, but he did not notice them.

"What I have seen, others will see. It is folly to ignore it."

Hendrick sat like stone at the table. Master Gregor watched Lord Leonard with narrowed eyes. King Guillaume looked grave. Councilors to either side glanced at her and back to Lord Leonard.

"To reward Master Gregor with such an honor—to make him a *duke*—will only make souls wonder how it happened that the young master just happened to be just there, where he could help the princess escape. A double treachery, to connive with the duke and then to snatch the duke's prize."

"But he didn't," said Sylvie. Her voice rang with clarity, to her relief, and Lord Leonard goggled at her and seemed unable to speak.

She walked up to the table with the basket. "It was not Master Hendrick who helped me escape." Then she pulled open the basket. Snowfall climbed out. "It was Snowfall."

Everyone at the table was looking at the kitten, and Snowfall looked back. Her father looked almost on the verge of smiling.

"And I don't think that Snowfall wants to be a duke." She scowled at the thought. "Or rather, a duchess."

"Of course not," said King Guillaume. "Everyone knows that the cat becomes a margrave—or margravine."

Snowfall walked along the table to rub against his hand, purring, and all the table laughed.

Also by Mary Catelli

Writing And Reflections
Writing And Reflections

Standalone
Curses And Wonders
Dragon Slayer
Eyes of the Sorceress
Fever and Snow
Mermaids' Song
Sword and Shadow
The Book of Bone
Witch-Prince Ways
Dragonfire and Time
Enchantments And Dragons
Jewel of the Tiger
Over the Sea, To Me
The Dragon's Cottage
The Maze, the Manor, and the Unicorn
The White Menagerie
A Diabolical Bargain
Madeleine and the Mists
Magic And Secrets

The Lion and the Library
The Princess Goes Into The Forest
The Wolf and the Ward
The Witch-Child and the Scarlet Fleet
Treachery And Spells
Winter's Curse
Crow Curse
Free Passage
Isabelle and the Siren
Journeys And Wizardry
Lifestone
Magic of the Lost God
Never Comment On A Likeness
One Name
The Drunken Mermaids
The Turtle in the Sea of Sand
Were I You
Where There Is Smoke
Through A Mirror, Darkly
The Princess Seeks Her Fortune
Oath Keeper
Queen Shulamith's Ball
Ripening Gold
Sorcery and Kings
The Firemaster and the Flames
The Hall of the Heiress
Spells in Secret
The Other Princess
The Enchanted Princess Wakes
Even After
Sylvie's Escape

About the Author

Mary Catelli is an avid reader of fantasy, science fiction, history, fairy tales, philosophy, folklore and a lot of other things. (Including the backs of cereal boxes.) Which, in due course, overflowed into writing fantasy (and some science fiction).

www.ingramcontent.com/pod-product-compliance
Lightning Source LLC
LaVergne TN
LVHW020048110826
845155LV00029B/685